I0597743

Shifting Scenes

ALEX SOTTO

SHIFTING SCENES

ISBN   978-1-64552-021-4   (Paperback)
ISBN   978-1-64552-022-1   (Digital)

Lettra Press books may be ordered through booksellers or by contacting:

Lettra Press LLC
18229 E 52nd Ave.
Denver City, CO 80249
1 303 586 1431 | info@lettrapress.com
www.lettrapress.com

THERE WAS NO letup to the winter. Winter was in full force as the polar vortex descended from the Arctic with howling winds. A cold snap had occurred throughout the week and caused devastating consequences throughout the city.

The homeless had been herded into shelters and the sidewalks were empty of strollers. There was more snow in the forecast, and the many inches of precipitation wreaked havoc in the streets and highways. There was a pileup of vehicles in Highway 401 which was reported in the news. Many were stranded in the roads as emergency crews sought to assuage the situation by towing cars out of the area. There were helicopters hovering above the roadways reporting the traffic situation to the listeners of radio and TV.

The news channels advised the residents to stay indoors, only to go outside if it was absolutely necessary. Nevertheless, schools were closed and there was no mail delivery. Children were in the park building snowmen and took their sleds with them to slide in the snow. Adults too were enjoying the frigid weather, taking out their ski gear and trying the low slopes of Mount Royal for an easy run downhill.

She was used to the messy mix of winter and was reclining in her bed under a warm woolen blanket. She was watching the icicles on her window pane and the copious amounts of snow that was falling. Her husband hadn't been home for three days and was wondering if he'd ever come back. She was in a fragile condition because she was two months pregnant.

Although she had taken the necessary precautions to ensure the health of the baby, she was beginning to have doubts whether she should keep the baby or terminate her pregnancy. Her marriage was on the rocks for reasons that were known only to her husband. She was twenty-three years old, and when she looked at the mirror, she saw a beautiful woman with blonde hair that reached her shoulders and aquiline nose that was a sign of her European roots.

How could her husband have abandoned her? What excuse could he have for wrecking their marriage? These questions were nagging in her mind and the only way to resolve this was to confront him.

Her name was Ava Dollins, and she was born and bred in Montreal. She was in no way going to be a single mother. She could not imagine raising a child singlehandedly without the love and support of the father of her child.

She met her husband at a party of an acquaintance. She had a few drinks and one thing led to another. Before she knew it, she had had some intimate moments with a man she hardly knew. She tied the knot a month later after she found out she was pregnant. Her mother did not even attend the civil ceremony because she argued that he didn't have a steady job. How could he support a family with the meager income he was earning?

Nevertheless, her faith in her husband was slowly slipping away. She knew she had made a wrong decision by going out with him that night. She was more than prepared to remedy the situation by going through some medical intervention.

By this time there was a knock on her door. It was Rosalie, her Filipino neighbor, who invited her for some coffee in her apartment. They had a lively conversation. Rosalie told her about her happy years in the Philippines without a single worry. She lived in a big farm in the southern part of the country, growing rice and sugarcane. The turning point in her life came when a new government was installed and implemented an agrarian reform law. The big tract of land that her family owned was taken away. They were left with only a few hectares, which was not enough to support a family.

Hence, she left the country and immigrated to Canada. Here she found a new home and a stable job that would make her self-sufficient. Later, Ava opened up to her and confided to her about her difficult situation. Her husband, Tommy, was nowhere to be found and left her with so many bills to pay. Her mother pitched in to pay the utilities and the rent while she used her savings to go about her daily life. She told Rosalie that she was planning to have an abortion. Rosalie was infuriated by what she said and pleaded with her to keep the child. Rosalie showed her a framed picture of her two children, now adults, whom she said brought her immense joy. "You'll regret it," added Rosalie and later informed her of a planned demonstration by the pro-life movement. "Be there," she counseled Ava, "it could very well change your mind."

The Philippines was a Spanish colony for three hundred years since its discovery in 1521 by Magellan until 1898 when Filipinos fought for independence. Spanish missionaries built churches all over the country and the indigenous people were baptized into the

Catholic faith. This explains the religious upbringing of Rosalie, who says the rosary every night before she goes to bed and attends Sunday mass every week. The Spanish language survives to this day in Zamboanga province where a patois is spoken and is a mixture of Spanish and native languages.

But Ava argued that she never married Tommy in church. Does this mean that they were living without the blessing of the church? Does this mean that their child would be born out of wedlock? Rosalie did not have all the answers to her questions. She merely encouraged her to go to church and talk to a priest who can enlighten her about the principles of the Catholic faith. Rosalie handed her a newsletter explaining the schedule of masses, the prayer intentions, and the address of the church.

At about this time, Rosalie's two daughters entered and kissed their mother. Rosalie pointed out that children are a blessing from God and wouldn't know what to do without them. Children will look after their mother once they reach adulthood. You can always rely on them to give you a helping hand. Ava bore all this in mind and said she might drop by the church since the church was not far away.

It was a mild morning in March when Ava headed out the door and went to the rally of the pro-life activists. The leaves in the trees had not quite sprung out yet but the sparrows on the branches were chirping. The ice on the sidewalks had begun to subside and the snow had considerably shrunk. The St. Patrick's Day parade had gone to a good start as onlookers lined the streets wearing anything green to signify the Irish heritage of the city. The pubs were full of the festive atmosphere as patrons drank green beer. There were Scottish men wearing kilts and playing bagpipes. The played a lively tune that turned the parade into a musical extravaganza. There were many people marching, holding banners and flags that represented the many guilds and societies in the city. There were many floats, but one float in particular carried the queen of the festivities. She was a fair-skinned woman who wore a crown and a flowing green cape. She waved at the well-wishers and beamed at the warm noonday sun.

But in another part of town, more specifically the Jeanne- Mance Park, there was another assembly that was taking place. There were hordes of women with children in tow who congregated around an improvised stage with two large speakers. Ava elbowed her way into the front of the stage to better hear what the speakers were saying. First up was the organizer of the rally, Anna Bouchard, who implored the government not to subsidize abortion services because this led to the degradation of women and violated the rights of the unborn children. She said that fetuses were a separate entity and had a right to a whole new life ahead of them. She also expounded on the risks women take due to the unhygienic conditions of some of the clinics. She wanted a reversal or the annulment of the Roe vs. Wade decision which legitimized abortion practices in North America. The crowd roared with approval on this one. Ava did not know what to make of the speech. Either she was too embarrassed to protest or if she would nod approvingly.

The next speaker was Sister Agnes from the Order of the Grey Nuns, whose convent sat at a hilltop in the outskirts of the city. She started her discourse by showing pictures of aborted fetuses whose frail bodies were mutilated by forceps and suction tubes. She pleaded with mothers not to go to abortion clinics but instead to lay their infants at the steps of the convent to be given to loving families who are eager to adopt them. There can never be enough children in this world. Their laughter evokes the time of innocence which we all lost because of the advent of puberty.

She pointed out that abortion cannot be easily forgiven by the church because it is a grievous sin. It requires restitution and long hours of community service because you took away the life of an unborn child. She asked nonpracticing Catholics to come back to the church, there to be guided to lead good spiritual lives. She ended her discourse by praying for each and every one assembled that they may receive the wisdom and guidance from the heavens above.

At this note, the rally ended. Workers started dismantling the poster and the banners. They also loaded the loudspeakers into the van. The crowd dispersed and went in many directions. But Ava remained unconvinced after listening to the two speakers. Why would she want to keep the child of a man who didn't love her back? Why would she want to burden herself when she can enjoy life as a single woman? All these questions were gnawing in her mind as she sought answers to her doleful predicament.

She took aside Anna Bouchard and explained to her, her situation. She believed that women should have complete dominion over their bodies. Women should have access to abortion clinics, artificial contraception, and regular checkups with the gynecologist to monitor the situation. What about teenage daughters who become pregnant? Are they to miss out on school just because they made a mistake? Do they have to live with this error in judgment all their lives? What about the situation in the world today where there is a shortage of food in a rapidly increasing population? Food production can simply not compete with the population growth. The famine in Africa is proof that there are children starving out there and they need immediate assistance from aid agencies and affluent countries. Doctors have to step in to control population growth and one of the ways is to perform abortions due to the high infant mortality rate.

Anna Bouchard was taken aback by what Ava said. Perhaps she attended the wrong rally and referred her instead to a pro- choice rally. Nonetheless, she told Ava that there was so much food wasted in North America. If they could only get those airlifts moving and dole out the food to the proper channels. She also told Ava that there were many couples out there who were trying to conceive a child and had gone to fertility clinics to no avail. She should count herself lucky to be pregnant for it fulfilled the elusive dream to be a mother. Being pregnant is a sign that the woman is of good health, and that she should not to take it for granted. Many women she knows would love to be in Ava's place, but due to a low sperm count or a malfunction in the ovaries they are not able to. It is a blessing to have a child, to nurture them and watch them grow. Children are to be cherished for a whole lifetime. After saying this she bade Ava goodbye and headed into the woods.

Ava turned to her left and saw a young woman lingering at the scene with two small children. Ava asked her if she was a single mother and she replied yes. Her name was Caroline Wozniak who was a brunette with hazel eyes. She was wearing a polka-dotted dress with a pair of blue slacks underneath and a sweater on top. She was artificially inseminated with her dead husband's sperm who died in mortal combat in Afghanistan. The procedure didn't take more than an hour and she did this because she loved her husband so much. She insisted her husband make a deposit of semen at the sperm bank because she feared for his safety. If anything happened, she could always ask the help of medical technologists so she could bear him children. She wanted to preserve the legacy of her husband, who was given a state funeral with complete military honors. Her husband was accorded the highly coveted Medal of Honor that was given posthumously. Caroline invited Ava to stroll down the park together and asked her to lead the hand of one of her toddlers. She said she had big plans for her children, especially now that she received a lump sum from the government as part of a compensation package to widows of fallen soldiers. Her husband's name would live on and she would always visit the Tomb of the Unknown Soldier on Remembrance Day.

Ava asked her how she took care of her children and if it was physically taxing. Caroline answered that she would drop her children at the daycare center before she went to work. She had a steady job that gave her a lot of income plus the government reparation from her husband's untimely death. Ava explained to her that she was pessimistic about her own situation because her husband did not contribute anything to their marriage. His long protracted absences made her feel like she wasn't married at all. Caroline told her not to worry and find another man who was willing to take the challenge of forming a family. Ava was young and attractive and should not have any problem appealing to suitors. They went down to a grassy plain where men were teaching their dogs to fetch Frisbees. At this note, Caroline said goodbye to Ava and went her way.

Alone in her apartment, Ava was reading the newspaper when she chanced upon an advertisement from a fortune teller/ psychic named Wanda. She guaranteed complete confidentiality, 100 percent reliability, and of being an expert seer with regards to the future of financial matters and romance. Ava dialed the number and an appointment was set up. The following day, Ava was in the bureau of Wanda, who wore big beads around her neck, a pair of boar-tooth earrings, and was of African descent. Ava was seated on the table across Wanda which had astrological charts, tarot cards, and a crystal ball at the center. There were also newspaper clippings on the table. Wanda asked her for her birthdate. To which Ava replied April 17. Immediately, Wanda drew her astrological chart and consulted with some of the books dealing with the subject matter. She warned Ava that due to the presence of the planet Mars on her chart she was bound to have an unpleasant love life.

Wanda laid out the tarot cards and a bad card showed up which meant that her present husband had little regard for her. Ava then asked her if she should carry the child in her womb to full term or have an abortion. Wanda then told her to put her hands on the crystal ball to see if she could get answers. When Ava finally retreated her hands, Wanda started to get a reading. It was the face and body of an unborn child with the umbilical cord still attached to the navel. The child was pleading to be given a chance to breathe fresh air and to enjoy the sights and sounds of the world. It said that it was dark and mushy inside the womb and sometimes there were not enough nutrients. It longed to be cradled in the mother's arms, there to rest in swaddling clothes.

Ava was shocked by what she saw and heard. Her unborn child talking to her through a crystal ball. What can be more preposterous? Now if only Tommy could communicate with her and say with finality their situation.

Tommy Smith was a regular kinda guy with no lofty ambitions, just a good-looking Canuck with blond hair that reached his shoulders and bushy eyebrows that made his blue eyes sparkle. He liked to hang out with friends, riding motorcycles and driving fast cars at the racing circuit. He liked playing ice hockey wearing the number fifteen jersey and would hit the puck hard so that it would go to the net. He would sleep over with his buddies while watching the late-night show and munching on a pizza with a six-pack beer. He was a carefree boy, not so much mature for his age. His parents divorced when he was twelve and he didn't have a tranquil childhood, often staying from one aunt to another. He dropped out of high school and could never get a steady job. He valued his freedom and his time with his friends. He was never meant for a serious relationship and could never imagine being a dad. He was not the least bit in love with Ava and was sorry he got into this mess. He had affairs with several girls but they were all one-night stands. He only slept with them to get his rocks off. Maybe he could enroll in a training course and become a mechanic. He had, after all, friends in the auto industry. But for now, he was spending time with friends, pursuing a hobby that would not brighten his future.

Ava's condition was becoming more and more obvious. She was having a hard time trying to conceal her pregnancy away from the prying eyes of the public. The bulge in her belly was eliciting unsavory commentary from her neighbors. Who was that pregnant woman strolling in the park without a husband? Did she get pregnant by accident or did she forget to take birth control pills? Looks like she got laid in an orgy and didn't know which one did her in. All this talk irked her and she wanted to put all gossip to rest. Time was running out. She had to act fast. Not all doctors would agree to perform late-term abortions. If only Tommy would come to clarify the situation.

There was a knock on the door. It was Tommy. Right away Ava began to question him in an aggressive tone of voice, "Where have you been all this time? Don't you know I'm married to you? Level with me and tell me where we're headed." But her yelling didn't do any good. It came in one ear and out another. He said he just came to get his clothes and that he wasn't attracted to her. It was all over. He was packing his clothes in a suitcase when Ava confronted him with her situation. What to do with the baby? Why doesn't he face his responsibility? Be a man for once and atone for his transgressions. But Tommy was oblivious to his surroundings and told her he married her just because he got her pregnant. But Ava pleaded with him to stay and that they could work things out. Tommy was nonchalant and was heading for the door when Ava slapped him. As a reflex motion, Tommy pushed Ava away and her belly hit the sofa. Ava fell on the floor and her lower torso was bleeding.

Tommy left with his suitcase. A few minutes later, Rosalie came and saw the door ajar. She was perplexed by the eerie stillness of the place and called out Ava's name. There was no answer. She put down the tray of cookies she had brought and looked around. There in the living room she saw Ava on the floor unconscious. There was a massive amount of blood on the rug and Rosalie called the ambulance.

Ava woke up in the hospital. Rosalie was to the left while her mother and brother, Michael, were sitting to the right. Ava had a mask over her mouth, with intravenous tubes attached to her arm. The doctor came in with some bad news. Ava had lost the baby. The doctor had performed a caesarean operation to try and save the child but the blunt-force trauma to the head of the child was too severe and perforated the skull that the child died. The doctor said to give the uterus some time to heal and take extra vitamins and she could conceive another child. But Ava was glad she lost the baby. She was freed from the burden of a loveless marriage that caused her anxiety and mental anguish. She couldn't wait to get out of the hospital and start her life as a single person once again. Fit into those jeans and wear those body-hugging clothes, things she missed doing ever since she was in that delicate condition.

Her mother warned her to choose a better husband and why not sue Tommy for the damages he did. Ava told her mom that she was letting go of Tommy and was not interested in bringing Tommy to court. They simply were not compatible.

It was already spring and she had plans of celebrating her birthday. She would have a nice stroll in the park and see the tulips and dahlias blooming. It would be refreshing to lie down on the green grass and bathe under the sun while reading a book. The birds that had left would soon be back from their migratory cycle. The whooping cranes with their long necks and she would even feed the pigeons with bread crumbs. Green is the color of life and soon those branches that were bare in the winter would grow leaves again. She looked at life with a different lens now. She was brimming with hope and looked forward to a new day.

The day of the birthday party had arrived. The room was festooned with red ribbons and balloons of different colors. The long table had ten chairs of striped upholstery and at the center was a large bowl of fruits. Ava had painstakingly prepared the whole setting and the menu, which included pecan pie, lemon meringue for dessert, and cashew chicken as the main course.

The first to arrive was George Kropoulos, who was a fashion designer and a good friend of Ava. He had a store in the Upper East End where all the snobbish people live. It had two mannequins at the display window fitted with brocaded dresses and intricate laces that gave the impression that summer was here. The mannequins had straw hats, dangling brass earrings, and wore sandals at the feet. The store was opened by George and his long-lost partner, Tony Cordello, who died of an undisclosed illness. Every time George thought about his partner, he would have this sinking feeling and sob intermittently. Making the business flourish would be his way of showing dedication to the store. George had many clients, including beauty contestants who looked for gowns to wear for the big night. Other girls came in and expressed their preference. George would take out a sketching pad and draw the gowns according to their taste and specifications. He would sketch the contours, estimate the length of the dress, as well as the depth of the neckline. He also had embroidered dresses on the racks, as well as fur coats that he displayed during the winter. He also sold designer shoes and slippers. Some had tassels and were made with genuine leather, while others had stiletto heels according to the occasion.

It should be stated that the symptoms of Tony's illness included bloating, violet discoloration, and shortness of breath. Nobody knows how Tony contracted the disease except that he frequented bars and nightclubs. His death left George distraught and he could hardly find an outlet for his sadness except his work, which kept him occupied.

The next to arrive at the party were the Monroe twins, Reeva and Stella. They were horseback riders who would compete in sporting events. They excelled in show jumping and dressage. With their identical hairstyles it was hard to tell them apart. They had freckles, and their long strawberry blonde hair was done in braids. Sometimes they would wear ponytails that were neatly brushed under their helmets. They wore white breeches and long leather boots. They took care of their horses and fed them herbs and carrots.

One day Reeva fell down from her horse while making it canter. Luckily, she didn't break any bones. She just had a bad knee with bruises and was indisposed for two weeks. After several visits to a chiropractor, she was back in form.

Stella fell in love with a man once. But when she found out he was married, she quit seeing him. She didn't want to be called the other woman wrecking a marriage. She was depressed but riding horses lifted her up. It was her favorite pastime that took most of her attention and effort. A horse of theirs was euthanized. It got caught in the brambles and badly injured her legs while grazing on the ranch. It proved a very daunting test for the twins, who attended to the health and wellbeing of the horses.

They made it on the cover of a sports magazine. They were given in-depth interviews and explained to the readers the joy and challenges of horseback riding. They were so elated and delighted by the exposure. Due to popular demand, they opened a riding school teaching the young and the old the rudiments of riding horses. There were classes for beginners and intermediate riders. They were a household name in the town. Anyone who wanted to be an equestrian enrolled in their school.

Riding horses meant the whole world to them. They would go around North America in search of pedigreed horses sired by champions from the best stables. These horses brought them fame and glory by adding trophies to their wide array of titles. They were so adept at riding horses. Nothing could separate them from their horses.

The next to arrive was Nancy Harrison, a mother of two adopted children. She and her husband were already advanced in years and regretted not bearing children of their own earlier in their marriage. They would go around the globe just to adopt children. One in Haiti and the other in China.

They had a business in philanthropy setting up the Feed the Hungry Foundation. Their organization was far reaching and extended around the world. Through their programs on TV, they would collect donations through their 1-800 number and online. Last year alone they amassed more than two hundred million dollars. They would airlift relief goods to famine-stricken countries. They would build artesian wells so that communities would have clean drinking water. They would provide meals for schoolchildren and medicine for those who are ill. They collaborated with others who were expecting. But that chapter with Tommy was all over. It was now the time to heal the deep scars she incurred from her husband's wrath.

Still on the list of invited guests was Michael, the brother of Ava. Michael was five years younger, who brought a stationary bicycle as a present. Ava's mother decided to get pregnant with her second child after a long hiatus. She missed the cries of the infant and thought the house would be more complete with two children instead of one.

Michael thought that Ava could use some exercise to burn the hidden fat in her belly. He believed that physical fitness was a vital component to one's health. He was devastated with what Ava went through and thought he would give her a helping hand during the crisis. Michael was a successful computer programmer who could configure laptops so that they would go up and running. He learned his trade during the many years in high school. They had computer classes and each student was equipped with their own console. Michael was also a health buff who set up organizations to become a more effective arm for charity.

They never forgot how blessed they were to live in an affluent country. They wanted to reciprocate by giving a brighter future to the less fortunate. They were optimistic that with the intense fundraising they could feed all malnourished children. They would go around universities and business forums talking about the need for awareness of the sad plight of poor countries.

They wanted to inculcate the value of reciprocity to their children. To give back to the world what the country has done for you. They always said grace before eating their meals. Their children were growing up having all the amenities and comforts in life. For this they should be grateful.

Nancy and her husband were blameless before the law. They never siphoned off funds for their own personal enjoyment. They issued receipts event for the smallest donation so that their donors could claim tax rebates when they filed their income tax returns. They were awarded a papal recognition for their tireless efforts in helping to alleviate human suffering and hunger in the world. Ava valued their friendship because this brought hope to her gloomy existence.

During her high school days, Nancy would ask Ava to babysit the children. She could help herself with the food in the refrigerator. She did a lot of errands for Nancy like shopping for groceries, doing the laundry, or cleaning the house. All this while keeping an eye on the two children. Ava bided her time between her classes in high school and doing odd jobs like mowing the lawn, bringing the pets to the vet, or accompanying seniors to their appointments with the doctor. Ava scrimped just to get by. She would avoid going to beauty salons or watching movies. Nancy would entrust Ava with wads of money. In those days, Ava was so energetic and unattached.

But now Ava was brooding over the failure of her marriage. How could Tommy have let her down, pushed her violently against the sofa to lose the child? They spent hours in the gym lifting weights. He was a stout young man with light brown hair that was parted in the middle. When he was sixteen, he fell in love with a Nigerian exchange student. Her name was Kalifa and had wiry black hair which she tied with a red hairband. Michael was attracted to girls with dark skin. He thought they were exotic and sultry. He got excited watching them. But his mother disapproved of the relationship and told him to keep away from her. Somehow his mother had this boding premonition that the relationship would not last and turn sour. She was right most of the time, like in the case with Ava. Besides, they were just too young for such a thing.

The mother couldn't figure out what went wrong with her children's upbringing. One because he was crossing the racial barrier, hanging around with creatures of an inferior race. The other because she got involved with a man of poor economic standing. They were after all a well-to-do white family and she expected her children to fare better in life. Her children were endowed with good physical attributes which were highly regarded by the print media and movies. They could easily have become actors starring in blockbuster films. Instead they chose the low life, dealing with people of the low caste.

The last to arrive at the party was Joe Kinsey. He was passing by Montreal on his way to buying a tractor. He was a farmer who owned a big orchard in the Eastern Townships, Quebec. His orchard was planted to orange trees and corn. He hired foreign labor from Central America and facilitates the working permits of his workers. He pays his workers well and hasn't encountered any problems with them. He has been a friend of Ava's family since way back.

His oranges were destined for the refineries of a famous juice company. He owned a lot of vehicles, especially the ones that are used for the harvest. He used only government approved pesticides to kill the bugs and the larvae of insects. And besides, he only used pesticides sparingly so as not to infiltrate the fruits and produce with too Reeva warns Michael that getting thrown off a horse is dangerous because you can break your spinal cord and result in paralysis. You'll be confined to a wheelchair all your life. Michael agreed to visit the ranch. But before he can mount the horse, he has to sign a waiver indicating that all safety precautions have been taken, and if anything untoward happens it won't be the fault of the ranch.

Meanwhile, Nancy Harrison and George Kropoulos were having a lively conversation. Nancy wanted George to do the interior design of her house. The couch in the living room was worn out, with the throw pillows in faded blue. He can even change the gray rug to a colorful Persian carpet. The curtains have to be replaced with venetian blinds to let the sunshine in with one flick of a finger. The upholstery of the bar stools had to be redone. So too with the fireplace, which needed a makeover. She needed new appliances in the kitchen with timers and thermal control. And the beds and the night tables in the rooms needed a major overhaul. Nancy had all these ideas and wondered whether George could come up with suggestions. George will many chemicals. He is planning to go to Florida in the summer to upgrade his farming techniques. He says farmers in Florida are so fortunate to have the sun all year round. When winter comes, Joe has to board up the place and stall his operation. His trees and crops go in hibernation when the frost comes. He plans to diversify by adding livestock to his business. This way he can earn a little more money by selling pasteurized milk.

His cottage is powered by solar energy. Later on, when he has cows, he'll use the manure as a biodegradable source of energy. He won't have to pay utilities anymore since he'll be independent. In an enterprise as big as this, one has to find ways of being self- reliant. He always tells Ava not to depend on anyone, especially since her last marriage was a sham. Better to be alone than in bad company. Joe offered Ava a job in the farm. Looking after cows, making sure they're fed, their pens are tidy, and milking them every morning. But Ava prefers the city life with all the tinsel, street lights, and the busy traffic. She'll be bored to death with such staid scenery and farm animals. She liked to take the subway with their cozy seats and automatic doors, passing by musicians playing their instruments and begging for alms. She felt great being at the hub of so much activity, her high heels making so much noise as the crosses the pavement. She looked at the store windows admiring their merchandise. These things she can't do at a farm. She politely turned down the offer.

The guests exchanged pleasantries. After a hefty serving of roast chicken, the guests helped themselves with the dessert. There was cake and ice cream. A little later, a birthday cake was brought to the fore with the number of candles corresponding to Ava's age.

She couldn't blow all the candles at once. She did it on the second try. Joe asked Ava if he could open the window since it was getting musty and to let some fresh air in. He could never adjust to the hectic atmosphere of the city. He longed for the wide, open spaces of the countryside. Already he was showing signs of homesickness. As he looked down, there was a commotion on the street.

Paramedics arrived and treated a badly injured woman. She got run over by a car and her bag of groceries spilled on the street. There was only a slim chance of her surviving. This is what happens when you live in areas of high density. People get crushed like sardines. So unlike the countryside where you can relax in a hammock and drink freshly squeezed oranges.

Reeva Monroe motioned to Micheal to come closer. She offered him free riding lessons at the ranch. Michael says he has ridden before but had dreams of participating in the Calgary Stampede. He'd like to ride a bronco kicking and bucking and try to hang on to the saddle. That would be a worthwhile adventure. But there was a mechanical horse in the ranch that gyrates back and forth. Perhaps he'd like to practice on that one before he rides the real thing. The horses in the ranch were already trained, so there was no need to use spurs or lassoes. Just a light nudge on the belly and the horse starts to trot. have to see the house and gives her a tentative date for the visit.

The transition from fashion designer to interior decoration shouldn't be hard. They're related fields. One deals with designing dresses while the other embellishes the surroundings. George has travelled extensively to Europe. Especially in France and Italy where designers there have creative uses for leather, suede, and other fabrics. He had a wealth of knowledge for the current tendencies of designing. He can turn a room of drab colors into an awesome hideaway.

The party was over. The guests headed out the door one by one, giving Ava a peck on the cheek and wishing her a speedy recovery. Ava turned off the lights and slept.

A week later, Rosalie visited Ava and inquired about her health. She was so concerned about the well-being of Ava that she brought a bottle of analgesic pills to ease the pain. She also taught Ava how to say the rosary and told her to recite it whenever she was assailed by doubts and apprehension. Before leaving, Rosalie suggested that she take a trip to the Philippines for a vacation and a change of scenery. Ava can stay with Maria Mendez, the cousin of Rosalie, who owns a small farm in the southern part of the country. She can get acquainted with another part of the world that she has never seen before. Ava accepts the invitation and intends to go there in July.

Ava flew to the Philippines wearing a short-sleeved shirt, jeans, and sneakers. Maria Mendez fetched her at the airport. It wasn't hard to recognize Ava. She with the long blonde hair and aquiline nose. They both rode a connecting flight to Panay Island, to a small town nestled between low mountains. The greenery was such that Ava exclaimed how breathtaking it was. They passed a long stretch of rice paddies and sugarcane plantations until they stopped at a one-story house with a teahouse of thatched roof at the front. There were roosters crowing and ducks flapping their wings in the front lawn. In the distance there were water buffaloes being used by barefoot farmers plowing the fields. She admired the rustic scenery and wished to see more. But now it was sunset and she must be tired from the trip. Maria plans to tour her around the place in the coming days.

After a good night's sleep, Ava was up and about, excited about what to do in the coming day. Maria served her pancakes, bread and butter, which filled her up.

Later in the day, Maria brought Ava to see some cockfighting. There was a red and a white rooster in the opposite corners of the ring. Both were fitted with sharp and deadly blades at the talons so that when they attacked each other they would inflict deep wounds to their bellies. A man was inside the ring collecting all the bets. Some bet on the red rooster while others vouched for the white rooster. Ava covered her eyes with her hands because she couldn't bear to see so much blood splatter. "This is a gory and sadistic sport. How could people be so cruel?" she thought to herself. Eventually, the red rooster won because it was lithe and agile while the white rooster was heavy and clumsy. The white rooster was dead on the spot. Its limping body was full of blood and gashes. The handler made the red rooster do a winning peck over the head of the lifeless white rooster.

Two days later, Maria brought Ava to the main thoroughfare of the town to behold the parade of beauty candidates. They all had flowers in their hair: hibiscus, fragrant jasmine, and red roses. They rode atop horse-drawn carriages. The luckiest one was to be crowned the flower queen. They passed through the street in colorful gowns. Some wore pink and other in blue and green. They all wore tiaras on their heads. The fairest one will be awarded a crown of pearls with glistening rhinestones.

Three days before Ava's departure, Maria hosted an extravagant lunch for her. Neighbors came, so did gatecrashers who heard from word-of-mouth that there was going to be a feast at the front yard of the house. It was not uncommon for uninvited guests to come meandering down to a fiesta since many people only had two meals a day and they were hungry. And since the gate was unlocked, people just rushed in.

There was a roasted pig at the center of a long table resting on banana leaves. Its skin was crunchy while the meat was pale, soft, and delicious. The called the main course a *lechon*, which had a gravy sauce to go with that. Then there were fried spring rolls which were stuffed with bean sprouts. Everyone liked to munch on them. Then there was a mélange of vegetables like okra and eggplant dipped in shrimp paste. They called this dish *pinakbet*. It had a pungent aroma that you had to get used to. To top it all was white rice, which the guests ate heartily.

One of the guests approached Ava, a man in his twenties, and told her that she was the fairest woman he had ever seen. He introduced himself to her and asked her if she could go to the town with him and have coffee. Ava declined and said she was busy packing up. The young man immediately fell to his knees and asked for her hand in marriage. Ava could hardly believe what she heard and told him that she barely knew him. The young man was persistent and pleaded with her to take him wherever she was going. He asked Ava if there were many blondes in her country. Ava was reluctant to reply. Ava was honest with him and told him that he was playing a prank on her. All he wanted was to come to Canada to escape the misery in his country. He should be proud of his beautiful country. Ava waved her hand and told him to leave.

As the festivity was winding down, Maria introduced a small girl to Ava. She was wearing a dress with floral prints and pink slippers. Maria told her she was an orphan because her mother died of childbirth complications. She didn't have a name yet and hadn't been baptized. The small girl needed a home. Ava jumped at the idea with enthusiasm and volunteered to take her to Canada where she will be adopted by a loving family. Ava had Nancy Harrison in mind, her friend engaged in philanthropy. She hugged the infant in her arms and told Maria she would have a brighter future in Canada. Maria acceded to Ava's decision and prepared the small carry-on luggage of the little girl, which included a teddy bear and some clothes.

Ava thanked Maria for the hospitality and off she went to the airport with the little girl. Upon arriving in Montreal, Ava phoned Nancy to come and fetch the toddler. Nancy was so overjoyed by what she saw and quickly called her Annabelle. She would have her own room in the house and she'll fill her closet with toys, dolls, and dresses.

It was noontime when Michael arrived at the ranch of the Monroe sisters. Reeva didn't see him right away because she was busy giving lessons to five students. Michael came closer to the paddock and hollered out her name. Immediately, Reeva dismounted from her horse and instructed her students to continue without her. Reeva led Michael to the stables and made him pick his horse. Michael chose a white horse that had been feeding on hay. Reeva put the saddle on and taught Michael how to adjust the stirrups. She gave him a helmet as a precautionary measure. And off Michael went to join the other students in Reeva's class. The horses were trotting around the paddock when Reeva motioned to the students to halt. Reeva said that this was a preparatory course to a future trail riding around the town. Reeva told them never to use a whip, because this will just disorient the horse. They were not in a race anyway.

Stella meanwhile was giving a horse a bath and brushing the mane to get rid of excess dandruff. She let the other horses graze in the field under the hot noonday sun. A ranch hand came and told Stella to bring the horses in the stable so they could drink some water. Their throats should be parched by now. Stella relented and instructed him to make sure there was enough grass to feed the horses. Horses, after all, were herbivores.

After an hour of riding horses in the paddock, Reeva instructed the students to dismount for the class was over. They brought the horses to the stable and removed the saddles. Michael was a fast learner and did everything Reeva told him to do. But Michael, with his penchant for dark women, was gravitating toward a black female student whose name was Anita. She was a tall woman with long black hair. He struck a conversation with her, commenting on how sleek and graceful she looked on top of a horse. He liked her good posture and poise while maintaining a safe distance from the other horses. He asked her if she ever rode a horse at a greater speed. Anita replied that riding horses was just a hobby and had no intention on participating in competitions.

Over a cup of coffee and some doughnuts at Tim Hortons, Anita asked Michael if he had been riding for a long time. Michael replied that it was his first day. He too had no intentions of pursuing a career in horseback riding. It was just to pass the time away. But he asserted that he was lucky to meet a girl like Anita because she brought out the man in him. He kissed her hand and asked if he could see her again. Anita warned him that she was not a loose girl and that he shouldn't rush her. In due time, she'll know if they were a match.

It was a cool September afternoon when a lot of people went to St. Stephen's church for the baptism of Annabelle. A whole slew of distinguished personalities had been asked to stand as godparents by Nancy Harrison. Ava came too since she was, after all, the bridge that brought the little girl and Nancy together. The officiating priest was Fr. John Rifkin, who was dressed in a flowing white robe with a golden cross and a dove at the center. He poured holy water over the head of tiny Annabelle and asked the godparents to join him in prayer.

There were eight godparents: four men and four women. Leading the pack was Richard Avery, a distinguished film director whose most recent movie earned him an Oscar nomination. He was dressed in a coat and tie and promised Nancy his unwavering support for her campaign. She would put blue kettles at the turnstile of movie houses to collect spare change for her fundraising. Some of the profit from his movies went to Nancy's programs for the needy. Nancy thanked him profusely.

Next was Dr. Donald Rothenburg, who was a general practitioner and a family doctor of Nancy's family. Two weeks ago, Annabelle came for a check-up and was given a clean bill of health. Sometimes Dr. Rothenburg would be assigned at remote locations to do a diagnosis of a stream of indigents. He would do a routine check-up and prescribe medications. It was all for the benefit of Nancy's charity.

Next in line was George Kropoulos, whom Nancy met at Ava's birthday party. He designed the dress that Annabelle wore at her baptism. The toddler wore a white long-sleeved dress and a see-through veil. She also wore white leather shoes that matched her dress. George also decorated the altar with white dahlias, the color of purity.

Rounding up the list of male godparents was Gerald Dalton who was an MP for Scarborough-Toronto. He was a topic of debate a while back for his controversial statements regarding the sovereignist party of Quebec. He called for the abolition of the separatist party arguing that it is no longer feasible due to the healthy economy of Canada.

He says that Quebec is better off as a province of Canada because of the numerous benefits it reaps from the confederation. He also thinks that Canada is doing a good job by granting autonomy to Quebec in matters concerning education, language laws, and immigration. This view boosted his support from the country's electorate. He met Nancy because they had the same circle of friends. Nancy was busy lobbying for more support from the government, and since he was in charge of the federal budget, they naturally crossed each other's path. Under Gerald's supervision, the government allocated funds for charitable institutions. It was not as big as the defense budget or the funds reserved for the upgrade in education and bursaries, but it was a considerable sum nonetheless. One thing he wished, however, was to find a wife and have children. At forty years old, he still hadn't found the right woman. Due to his busy schedule, he hardly had the time to go on dates. Maybe this was his chance. He was eyeing Ava with her long hair and svelte figure. Maybe during the reception he could sit beside her and get to know her.

Heading the list of godmothers is Emma Zamboni, an Italian expatriate who owns the restaurant Al Dente, which is a favorite haunt of Nancy. The restaurant specializes in the serving of spaghetti with oysters, tomato sauce, and meatballs. It also offers lasagna, fettucine carbonara, and tortellini. The chefs come from Italy, where they were trained to do some authentic Italian cuisine. They only use olive oil and the best aromatic herbs. She was planning to branch out to the rest of Canada to consolidate her multimillion-dollar enterprise. Right now her restaurant will serve as the reception for Nancy's entourage after the baptism. Nancy has always liked eating pasta. She has spaghetti almost every day. But she could never get the right texture from her tomatoes. She wanted to make the sauce herself. She asked Emma how to prepare the tomato sauce. Emma told her to put some herbs, add olive oil, and to boil it to a certain degree. Nancy thinks she has got it right this time. But she's still a regular at Emma's restaurant.

The next in the lineup of female godparents was Monique Bovette, a politician within the ranks of the Independence Party of Quebec that advocates for the separation of Quebec from the rest of Canada. She met Nancy through a mutual friend and was so impressed with the fundraising skills of Nancy that she enlisted as an auxiliary of Nancy's team.

Gerald Dalton spotted Monique at the church grounds and immediately asked her why she was at a federalist stronghold and at a christening of a Filipino child since he thought all separatists were racists. Monique reminded him that they were in Quebec and that she was present to welcome the child to Quebec society.

She argued that Quebec was becoming more culturally diverse and that meant training children to embrace the French culture and teaching the French language in their early years. The independence of Quebec was their main goal but that didn't mean they couldn't mingle with people of other racial origins. On the contrary, to become relevant to the times, the party has had to recruit militants from various cultural communities.

Gerald reiterated that breaking up the country was a serious matter. That Monique Bovette should just dissolve her party so that Quebec can attract investors and realign the province with the rest of Canada. Monique retorted that Quebec had a right to chart its own destiny. Quebec politicians have the duty to protect the French identity from the massive onslaught of Americans. Our ties to France have to be strengthened to preserve the legacy of our forebears. As this was being said, Nancy told them both to lower their voices as the baptismal rite was about to commence.

The third in the list of godmothers was Jacqueline Cazelle. She was the curator of the Montreal Museum of Fine Arts and recently ran an exhibit of the works of renowned painter Jean Dagenais. He was a homegrown painter who illustrated the landscape of Quebec and the interior of cottages onto the canvas. Some of the paintings featured in the exhibit came from the private collection of Nancy Harrison.

Jacqueline had a chat with Nancy before the ceremony and said that she was contemplating mounting an exposition featuring antique vases and pottery. She wondered out loud whether Nancy could contribute any of these to the exhibit. Nancy replied in the affirmative and said she'd pack her collection in crates with Styrofoam and send it to the museum. Jacqueline also asked Gerald Dalton if he could exempt the incoming shipment from tariffs since it would serve the interests of the general public. Gerald would gladly look into the matter and gave her his calling card to keep in touch in the coming days.

The last godmother was Barbara O'Connor, who was the branch manager of Strathmore Bank. Nancy had a commercial account in the bank and deposited large sums of money from time to time. She asked Nancy if she was going to use the same account number for her Christmas drive since this would greatly augment the revenue of the bank. Nancy told her not to worry since she had only one commercial account. Make all checks payable to the foundation and the bank would issue the receipts.

Barbara inquired what all the fuss was about between the Independence Party candidate and the MP from Scarborough. Nancy said that they were just having a discussion about politics. Nancy reminded everyone that the baptism of her daughter should not be a political forum where you can promote your beliefs. There are venues where you can properly express your opinions and get coverage from the media. As it is now, the press is calling the whole affair a circus event due to the harsh exchange of words.

The baptismal rites were in progress. The little child bent down facing a bowl made of marble as the reverend father poured holy water on her head. "May the hallowed halls of this church bear testimony to the entrance of this new member of the flock into the Catholic Church," uttered the priest. He gave instructions to the godparents to never let down the aspirations of this fledgling and to guide her every step of the way. May she never stray from the path of righteousness and may she share her love with the rest of humanity. May the godparents shield her innocence from malignant forces and nurture her spiritual life with good intentions. The priest made the sign of the cross on her forehead using consecrated oil. The priest then instructed the godparents to hold a lit candle and to take the oath of allegiance. "I, your name, do solemnly swear to defend the spiritual growth of this little girl, Annabelle Harrison, so that no evil power may stain her immaculate soul which is now purified from original sin. From this day forward, I will endeavor to be a good influence on her life and adhere to the tenets of the Catholic Church." The priest then concluded the baptismal rites and told them they could extinguish their candles. The priest shook the hands of all the godparents and told Nancy she had the greatest responsibility of all which was to turn her home into a haven of peace and goodwill. Nancy thanked the reverend father and led them all to the waiting limousines which were to drive them to the restaurant for the reception.

At the restaurant, Ava was seated adjacent to Fr. John Rifkin. She initiated a dialogue that began like this:

"I have no compunction over the life of the unborn baby. I considered having an abortion until the unexpected turn of events where there was an attempt on my life. Due to the traumatic shock that I endured, I naturally lost the baby. I have no regrets losing the baby, and I must say that I was relieved of the outcome."

Fr. Rifkin replied, "You are apparently a confused girl. It was not your fault that you lost the baby. You committed no sin in that regard. We here at the church would like to give valuable counseling to people who have lost their way. It is important that you read the Bible and be informed about the teachings of the church. We at the church have to defend the sanctity of human life. We have to teach mothers to value the gifts God gave and appreciate the abilities that are part of your nature.

"Giving birth is a miraculous event. From the long and arduous gestation, you are suddenly faced with a joyous milestone where from the portals of the human flesh, you will give birth to a newborn baby. It is a time of much rejoicing where all the effort of being a mother is fulfilled. The role of a woman is to propagate the human race so that the whole world will be teeming with life. A barren woman is a curse to society because she can no longer accomplish the role that was made for her. Look at the animals that breed in this world. They all have numerous young to ensure the survival of their species. Their nipples are overflowing with milk so that their puppies, cubs, or kittens are well-fed. It is the same with humans who are destined to multiply in their own image."

"But why does the church have to intrude into people's lives? Isn't it enough that the church give people free rein in matters concerning their existence?" Ava interjected.

"Because man is bound to commit mistakes. The church is the good shepherd who looks after the flock so that they don't fall by the wayside. If the church were to fall silent in crucial matters such as childbirth, then women wouldn't reap the rewards of being a mother. We at the church would like to raise awareness of the importance of being a mother. That is why the Virgin Mary occupies a special place in the church. We want to emphasize the pivotal role of the Virgin Mary in the doctrines of the church. She is the Mother of God who intercedes for us in our relationship with her Son. We recognize the crucial role mothers play in the upbringing of their children. If mothers were to terminate their pregnancy, then the world would be sorely lacking of children.

Mothers drive the economy to prosper by providing much-needed labor.

The youth propels the country forward. If there were a shortage of young people, then who will run the country?"

But Ava was adamant and stuck to her contention. She said, "But many women nowadays are averse to having children. They give priority to the advancement in their careers, putting marriage in the backburner, and prefer to enjoy their status as single persons rather than having the burden of staying at home to watch over their infants."

"In that case," the priest asserted, "let women then lead the life of single blessedness. May they exude holiness in all its forms whether they are by their lonesome selves or in the company of friends.

"If a single woman exhibits a vocation for prayer, let her seek a higher realm, a circle of likeminded women so that she can grow in a positive light. There is always the option of joining a nunnery or convent where single women are recruited to fill the declining staff. Widows and women in distress can find solace by entering the confines of an abbey where they will be greeted with a tranquil spirit.

The doors are always open to new recruits because it is one voice more to sing praises to God.

"We were all created in the image of God and we must make every limb of our body to praise the goodness of God. You are still young and have not fallen to the lower depths. But you can trust in God and see this invisible hand rescue you from destruction. Learn how to pray so that you many not succumb to the wiles of the devil."

"How do I know if I have a religious vocation?" Ava interrupted.

"The mere fact that you are talking to me means that you want answers to your lack of faith. Do you go to church every Sunday?" the priest asked.

"No, I don't. I don't have much of a religious upbringing. I might as well attend one Sunday to see if it's right for me," Ava continued.

"I can see that you are unsure of yourself. Go to church because it is worth your while. I assure you that you will be enlightened by the service. Listen intently to the gospel and take heed of the sermon because what the priest says is relevant to the times. I think I've answered enough of your questions. If you'll excuse me I have other matters to attends to." With that, Fr. John Rifkin rose from his seat and left.

On the other corner of the table sat Richard Avery, the film director, in front of George Kropoulos. They were having an animated conversation over a glass of red wine. Richard Avery broke the ice and told George that he was hired by the local opera company to stage the opera "Madame Butterfly" by Puccini. He was looking for a designer who could make the costumes for the lead singers, as well as, the rest of the cast.

George firmly said, "I'm familiar with that opera and watched that opera various times on stage. I even have different recordings of that opera. I know that it is set in Japan and has a tragic ending with the suicide of the lead singer. I can very well design the kimonos of the female cast with taffeta and silk. A kimono is actually a loose robe with wide sleeves traditionally worn with a broad sash as an outer garment. I am familiar with most national costumes of the world."

"What about the costumes for the tenor and baritone?" Richard inquired.

"Silk is the fabric commonly used in Japan. The men usually wear robes fastened with velvet sashes. They're tied above the waist. The pants are loose fitting, tied with a garter, and made of the same fabric. I adore the opera "Madame Butterfly," especially if it sung by first-rate singers. The soprano is a demanding role who is present on the stage most of the time. May I ask who is the lead singer?"

"The soprano to sing the role of 'Madame Butterfly' is Galina Vorodovskaya. She is a Russian singer who has sung in the major opera houses of the world," affirmed Richard.

"In that case I have to take her measurements as soon as she flies into town. There will be several fittings to make sure the gowns are well-tailored. I've met several designers from Japan, and I am familiar with the way kimonos are made. I've drawn several sketches of the traditional Japanese dress and am excited to put them in practice."

"Rehearsals are to begin in two weeks, and I hope you have all the materials. You will have to take their measurements on stage while they're rehearsing. I do hope you have enough dressmakers to make the costumes of the entire cast," warned Richard.

"I have a whole battalion of dressmakers who will sew the clothes so that they turn out to be one shimmering piece. I won't use any gaudy fabrics, just pastel colors that blend with the scenery. I can even put chrysanthemums on their hair so that when they sing the flower duet. It will be entrancing to watch. I hope you'll introduce me to the set designer. I am going to work in tandem with him. We have to iron out the kinks in the production. Nothing should stick out like a sore thumb. Everything has to blend smoothly. The costumes have to be in harmony with the surroundings," George enthused.

"He's a local boy who's been with us for two seasons now. I'm sure you'll find him receptive to all your suggestions. He'll cooperate with you so that the production moves on without a hitch," Richard said.

At this the two men shook hands and agreed that the name and picture, as well as, the credentials of George Kropoulos be printed in the program. It's a whole new window for the fashion designer who has always yearned to leave his imprimatur on the operatic stage.

On the far end of the table was Ava Collins who was eating a plate of spaghetti when the MP for Scarborough, Gerald Dalton, sat in front of her and began to talk.

"What's a pretty girl like you sitting all by herself in this crowded restaurant?"

"I'm a friend of Nancy who attended the baptism. My name is Ava, and I don't think I know your name."

"My name is Gerald Dalton who is one of the godparents at the baptism. You are like a magnet to me. I'm attracted to your good looks and wonder if I could spend some time chatting with you," Gerald pursued.

"I'm wary about entertaining male suitors since I just got out of a marriage with a man who was hostile and indifferent to me. What makes you different from the other men I came across?"

"I can see now that we'll make such a lovely pair. I am a government official who's looking for a lady who'll exude charm and grace to manage my household that until now is devoid of any feminine figure. I'll make you the queen of my riding. My constituents will bend their knee to you, and you will make my term in office a conjugal adventure that many will come to appreciate."

Ava was coy and unassuming and couldn't believe what she had just heard. It took time for her to digest all this unexpected whirlwind romance. After a while, she came to say, "I am impressed with all this romantic interlude. I don't know if I deserve this proposition from a high-ranking official. A handsome man like you should have many damsels to do his bidding. I am surprised that you come to me and offer me a place in your home. I have to think things out and see if you're the right man for me."

"In four years I will run for the office of prime minister. I need a woman who is willing to be the mother of my children. You seem to be of child-bearing age. Is your body ripe for motherhood?"

"I lost my baby due to unforeseen circumstances. I am willing to give motherhood a second chance. I will help you run your campaign so that voters will flock to you. A man who is single and bereft of any children is hardly the man that voters hope for. I don't want to do things in haste, but what do you expect in the days to come?"

"I want to ask your hand in marriage and make our union official. We'll go out of this restaurant together and make our vows as husband and wife solemnized by the church."

"It's going to take at least a month to plan. I still have to have a wedding gown made with the fashion designer. Aren't you going to slip a ring on my finger?"

"I will go to the jeweler and purchase the right ring for you. A diamond ring with matching earrings will surely make you rise to the occasion. I'll foot the bill for all your needs. You can move in with me anytime you want."

"I'll move in with you only after the marriage. Any ideas for our honeymoon?"

"We can fly to Europe and tour the whole continent. I can get us deluxe accommodations, and you can go shopping in the most exclusive boutiques," Gerald asserted.

"I look at my role as the wife of a politician with much trepidation and uncertainty. What do you expect of me?"

"Just stay as pretty as you are. You are to represent the nation wherever we go. Whether on tours abroad or hosting the visit of foreign dignitaries. You are to showcase the dresses of local designers and promote their creations to the spectators. Your flawless complexion and voluptuous hair will be an added advantage to your exposure. I'm sure you'll be the darling of the media because you're photogenic and downright stunning. You look like the Nordic, goddess of beauty straight from Scandinavian mythology. Where did you get those blue eyes and soft blonde hair?"

"Both my parents are of Anglo-Saxon ancestry. I had freckles when I was small, but they whittled away when I grew up. When I was a child, I wasn't exactly pampered with toys or dresses. I had to struggle to eke out an existence. I went to school with shoes one size bigger. And here I am faced with a prince charming ready to slip on my glass slippers."

"You will be riding on a gilded coach on your way to our wedding. I will be standing at the door waiting for you. You will be wearing a sapphire brooch on your breast that will bear the family insignia. All the eyes of the world will be on you as you will walk down the aisle in your wedding gown. I will put on your head a crown with twelve diamonds which will signify that you will have united with our family.

"I am a descendant of a long line of aristocracy. My grandfather was the earl of Stratford. Like you, I am proud of my Anglo-Saxon lineage.

I want my children to be a conduit for English traditions. To speak a language that has been handed down from generation to generation. You will be the light that will guide the culturally diverse population to adopt English as the language of commerce and education."

"But how will we raise our children," asked Ava "when the city is crowded and the air is choking with smog and dust particles? Our children need a healthy environment where they will be surrounded by nature and enjoy the lush greenery."

"I have a duplex in a suburb of Toronto and a vineyard in the Okanagan valley. There is ample space in my domain enough for a growing family. I am a man of sufficient means. You will look no more than the confines of my estate to know that you are looked after. I will not venture into this affair if I knew that I would be lacking in resources."

"My mother would be so proud of me for marrying an English aristocrat. Unfortunately, my father is not around anymore to witness this event. He died ten years ago in a car crash," intimated Ava.

"My family owns vast landholdings in Canada. I stand to inherit a sizable fortune. I am only one of two heirs, the other being a sister of mine who has never married. I am sure my father will welcome you to our family, happy over the choice I've made. Even when I'm no longer in politics and I've shut down my campaign office, you'll still lead the life of a privileged few who will cruise to the islands of the Mediterranean in a yacht and dine using expensive silverware.

All I ask is that you bear me a son so that my name will go down in future generations."

"It's good that you found me in the nick of time. Ten years from now, I'd already been a wrinkled prune. The real crown jewels are what's in my womb. I can bear the children you want for they are already bursting at the seams, ripe for the picking. With my racial background, I am the right genetic material for your offspring. You and I are an ideal match, made in heaven. We are to be wed in the church, for I won't have it any other way. My children will not be born out of wedlock. They will be legitimate heirs to your name and to your fortune," added Ava.

At this moment, an irate Monique Bovette rushed headlong to the table where Gerald Dalton was sitting and upbraided him over the comments he made earlier in the day. She started, "How dare you give me a lecture on the way the government should be run. Don't you know we've been in power for twenty years and not one citizen voiced an unfavorable opinion about us? The Independence Party is the voice of the Quebecois people, and we are a legitimate party who seeks to further the course of sovereignist-minded people. We will not acquiesce to the brazen demands of English lawmakers that we shut up and accept whatever legislation they propose. We have to defend the interests of the French-speaking population. French is the only official language of Quebec, and we have to promote the French language in every nook and cranny of this province. We have taken into account that independence is the only way to achieve the supremacy of the French language, which is why we will fight tooth and nail just to achieve it. Those militants in my quarters might deal a severe blow to your party due to the negative impact of your statements. Watch what you say because the Quebecois population is growing uneasy. You are fanning the flames of insurrection, and something unfortunate might happen to you."

Gerald riposted, "I am not going to take threats from you. As a member of a federalist party, it is incumbent upon me to create a country so that every province is woven into a coherent whole. All you sovereignists are doing is tearing this country apart. Canada is a bilingual country, and we respect the right of the francophone population to come up with legislation to defend the usage of the French language. But to become independent and establish a separate country will have repercussions with the rest of Canada. You can no longer use our currency, and you will have to pay tariffs for the goods that you will export. Your new country will have reduced economic ranking and will no longer have the clout it once had. On the contrary, if you stay within Canada, you will continue to receive government funding for all of your social programs."

"Quebec has the financial means to be an independent country," insisted Monique. "We have abundant natural resources, and our economy is sound without the double-digit inflation that continue to sink this confederation. We can very well go it alone without your help. We have plans of making the French-speaking nations a viable institution in the world stage. Our league of nations will surpass expectation, and we will be a force to reckon with. We will be friendly to our English-speaking neighbors, but we are committed to strengthening our ties with our French brethren. The English language is like noise to our ears. We don't want to be fed with slang words and a culture that is uncouth and lacking in sophistication. We don't want to genuflect before the English monarch who deprived us of our right to independence. We want our own separate homeland that will make laws for the benefit of our citizens. We can maintain our standard of living without your interference. So stop meddling in our affairs because we're fed up with you."

Ava clasped her hands and prayed that the heated exchange of words between her husband-to-be and the Independence Party candidate would stop. They were screaming at the top of their voices. It left the dining area in disarray as the invited guests and customers were horrified by the verbal assaults one dealt with the other. Monique splashed a glass of water at Gerald, and this provoked Gerald to slap Monique. Monique gushed forth a barrage of insults directed at Gerald. By this time, security was called in, and they dragged Monique out of the dining area and ejected her from the restaurant. She was repeating to Gerald that he was going to pay for all the damage he'd done to the separatist cause.

Nancy went to Gerald and apologized for all the panic that Monique caused. She wondered if he suffered any bruises or cuts due to the melee. Gerald said he sustained some scratches to his face because Monique physically attacked him. Nancy told Gerald that he should never have berated Monique at church about her separatist ambitions because that only instigated the confrontation. But Gerald replied that he approached Monique only to defend the unity of the confederation. The separatist cause is like a cancer that is eating up the country. The ones who promote it should be held accountable and stopped on their tracks. Nancy reminded Gerald that the restaurant was hardly the venue for such a controversial topic, and he would do better if he brought it up during election time. Nevertheless, the troublemaker had been ejected from the restaurant, and the atmosphere of the place became more serene and convivial. Gerald wiped himself dry with a napkin. Gerald broke the news to Nancy that he had found a bride and that it was none other than the buxom blonde Ava. Ava was still recovering from the turmoil and wiping away tears from the shocking incident. She looked around to make sure that the violent feline was nowhere in sight. As soon as she regained her composure, she acknowledged that she was indeed the bride-to-be.

Ava gave a short speech. "I am betrothed to a man who will not flinch from the challenges ahead. He has sacrificed his privileged life to serve his constituents in the most honest and truthful manner. He knows that there are hard times when the unity of our country is assailed by malevolent forces who seek to put our country in jeopardy. He has stated that he will work hard to defend the borders of our country so that no separatist party can break it up. We are fortunate to live in a vast country so that whoever should turn up on our shores should not be sent back but be given a chance to start a new lease on life. The only condition is that we abide by the law and that our actions be in conformity with the rules and regulations. As the better half of an elected official, I hereby declare that I will stand by the decisions of my husband because it is for the good of the country.

"The life of a politician is never easy. He is torn between the privacy of his home and the frenzied atmosphere of his office. I will spend my time having sleepless nights just so my husband can come up with laws that are beneficial to the general public. I will be attuned to the grievances of the people so that we can thresh out a plan to address them. If my husband is elected prime minister, we will widen the scope of deep-sea navigation so that we can unlock the wealth of minerals and natural resources and launch a subterranean exploration of oil and natural gas. We will no longer have to rely on imports from overseas refineries rather we will be self-sufficient on our energy needs. We will upgrade the safety of our railways so that the transport of oil and other volatile substances will pose no danger to the surrounding area. We will harness the potential wealth of the country in order to maintain our standard of living. All we ask is that everyone be alert to the shifting scenes of our times so that no one is left to deteriorate. We have at our disposal a vast amount of opportunities, and it is up to us to maximize our potential.

"With the leadership of my husband, we are on the road to attaining our dream. So let us choose the candidate who has the vision to put this country on its feet."

The crowd at the restaurant rose to their feet and gave Ava a standing ovation. Her speech was met with thunderous applause as everyone agreed that changes had to be made to the social and economic sector. Gerald stood up and raised his wine glass. He proposed a toast to the success of his forthcoming marriage to Ava. Later the restaurant clientele lined up single file to shake the hand of Gerald, to congratulate him for choosing a beautiful bride and for his incisive forays into politics.

Now one of those who offered felicitations to the gleaming couple was Susan Downer, a political science professor at Concordia University. She had dark hair, green eyes, and was on the plump side. She carried a notebook with all the annotations and markings of the day. It was like a diary where she described the events of the day. She asked if she could have a chat with the MP of Scarborough, and that person nodded.

She asked if he could do something about the protection of minority rights, especially when it came to furnishing services in English.

Hospitals are increasingly becoming hostile to English- speaking patients by issuing notices and memorandums in the French language only. Instructions to voters are being delivered exclusively in French which sows confusion on election day. Services at the municipal level and town hall meetings are being given in French and neglects the needs of the English- speaking constituents. Interviews at the welfare office are being done in French which leads to frustration among nonfrancophone recipients. The minimum wage is exceedingly low which leaves much to be desired.

Gerald brushed the sweat from his brow and straightened his tie. He replied, "Things will only get worse if Quebec becomes independent. There will be provincial election in two years, and according to the polls, the Independence Party is garnering enormous support from the masses. The French population is disenchanted by the way the government is run, especially in matters of immigration. They think that the province is being flooded with nonfrancophone immigrants who are diluting their identity and threatening their distinct character. Once they are reelected into power, the

Independence Party promises to hold a referendum on the future of their province."

"But isn't that illegal?" inquired Susan. "No single province should have a say on their future. Quebec does not have the power to secede unilaterally.

There has to be a consensus with the rest of Canada. Canada cannot sit idly by and watch a big chunk of their territory go to the hands of the separatists."

Gerald continued, "The only way is to defeat the separatists in the ballot box. By giving Quebec concessions like financing their solidarity programs and retirement plans, the Quebecois people should want to remain in Canada. But even with all this subsidy, the Canadian government can fail. My suggestion to you is to start an awareness campaign to all eligible voters that by remaining within Canada. We can sustain your lifestyle, deliver the package, and supply you with the necessities of life. This early, I advise you to start looking into livelihood prospects in other provinces so that when the unexpected happens, you'll be prepared to move." "That's not fair," cried Susan. "I moved to Quebec with my parents when I was nine years old. I know the streets of Montreal like the palm of my hand. I have many friends here. I've grown attached to the province but still want to keep my Canadian passport."

Gerald stated further, "The eventual secession of Quebec is a foregone conclusion. Nothing we do or say will make them change their minds. Remember that a large segment of the population was born in France, and they naturally want closer relations with the country of their birth. We can only entice them with grand projects to give up their dream of becoming a country. But the final say lies with them since they never agreed to any treaty."

Susan's eyes were downcast, and she was disappointed to hear about Gerald's unwillingness to change things. With a clenched fist she said, "I will fight to the bitter end. I will gather my forces and fix the lopsided treatment that English people are undergoing. I will correct this injustice and march in battle. English speakers will not be relegated to second-class status. The importance of English cannot be underestimated, and I will proclaim to all that we will keep our language even in the face of mounting adversity." With creases on his forehead, Gerald countered, "Quebec is not my jurisdiction. I am the MP for Ontario. You are most welcome to move to my province where you will be in the company of your ilk. You can move from this inhospitable terrain to a province that is more receptive to your likes and ambitions and a more culturally diverse province since there are no language laws that prohibit you from expressing your ideas."

Susan Downer stomped her right foot as a sign of dismay from her conversation with Gerald. She said she was not giving up her fight for equal rights, and she walked away bristling with anger.

Gerald and Ava too wrapped up their impromptu conference. They kissed Nancy and told her she'd be getting an invitation to their wedding. Ava took a last sip of water and exited the restaurant holding the hand of her beau.

Meanwhile, Michael and Anita were getting along very well. Michael thinks he could've gotten Anita pregnant due to frequent morning sickness. They were planning on getting married. Not a grand wedding due to their slim budget. Just a small gathering of the family and a few friends.

Michael tried inviting his mother, but when she found out the ethnicity of the bride, she mailed in a letter explaining her refusal. "Dear Michael," she started. "Much as I would like to be present at your wedding, I simply have to refuse because I object to your choice of a bride. I raised you within the confines of a loving home surrounded by people of your own racial background. Remember our Swedish neighbors who dropped by often so you could play with their children? Your classmates from high school who inducted you into their clubs for young Aryan teens? Why have you betrayed your roots and chosen to move in with a black pygmy? Surely you don't expect me to cradle your dark babies in my arms. I don't want you anywhere near primitive people least of all to have a wife who bears a resemblance to a gorilla. If you go ahead with your marriage plans to that half-baked creature, then I'll have to disown and disinherit you. I hope you understand the repercussions of your impulsive decisions which are not based on sound judgment. I regretfully have to decline your invitation." The letter was signed, "Your mother."

"Who needs her?" screamed Michael, an obvious reference to his mother. "I don't like people who speak ill of other races. I greet people with open arms whether they are Chinese, Japanese, or of African descent. You don't judge people by their appearance. For me, racial origin is immaterial. We all descended from a common ancestor. It's just that I have an affinity for dark skin color. To me they're exciting, and it whets my appetite.

"I have a Canadian mind-set, and I believe in multiculturalism. Canada is doing great accepting immigrants from the four corners of the world. Were it not for the increased levels of immigration, we would never have met. I am one of the most understanding and compassionate guys you'll ever meet. Never mind what other people think of us whether we're salt and pepper or cream and chocolate. We'll defy the odds and exceed people's expectations. My mother's point of view is out of step with the times. She's obviously living in a time warp when the fight for civil rights wasn't happening. She'll be in a shock when she finds out that the man in the passport office is black. You just can't wipe out the blacks from Canada anymore. They're becoming more and more prominent.

"Look at the newscasters, the basketball and hockey players, the cashiers at Tim Hortons. A lot of them are black. I will start a big family, and I will teach my children to hold their head high and never be ashamed of their racial background. We will brush aside the aunts and jeers of the oncoming rush of people. We will conquer the world by our equanimity and confidence. We will never shrink from the obstacles that lie ahead. This is the dawn of a new age when the white man will no longer hold the reins of power."

Anita just folded up in her chair like a rubber band. She was unperturbed upon hearing the contents of the letter. She has heard those snide remarks about her race before and refused to allow it to ruffle her feathers. When she came to this new land, she knew she would encounter surprises. She was well prepared for the many twists and turns that lay in store for her. She hardly expected a white man like Michael would come and court her. She was impressed though by the rigid stance of Michael against racism.

He was out of the ordinary rising like a knight in shining armor to come to the defense of his lady love. From now on there would just be the two of them astride in the rough waters of life. Anita knew she was a beauty of some sort never wincing her slender figure from the outrageous assaults of future transactions. She knew that if she was down one day, something would buoy her up to the surface the next time. The easier it is to breathe on the ground than at the bottom of the sea. Well, this was the moment, and she wasn't going to let it pass. She vowed to follow her husband wherever he went and not let their union be torn in half.

She was on solid ground now, and that meant a wide array of opportunities. She was far away from the swaying of the palm trees of her native Caribbean where she would just be reduced to doing the job of a lowly seamstress, a store clerk, or one who grounds cornmeal on a mortar. She would have none of that. She grew to cherish her adopted land even if it meant occasional name-calling. It was hard where she set her sights, a land where icicles would form a good part of the year. A place where the strong dollar would lift up everyone from the miasma of their otherwise sordid existence. She would utilize her talents to scratch the surface of the earth so that it would grow to giant sunflowers and lush greenery. She would let the stale air out and let the sunshine and fresh air in. She would no longer have to wear hand- me-downs and rubber slippers with holes on them. She would have a decent wardrobe with a variety of clothes that would suit the four seasons. She would no longer have to contend with beggars snatching her purse or street urchins mugging her in the corner as in her country of origin. Here indigents were given handouts from the government who looked after the welfare of its citizens. Canada to her was a respectable country where you hardly hear of muggings at night. Everyone was in the safety of their homes enjoying a meal of pot roast and a warm glass of milk before bed. There was no vandalism or graffiti on walls before the shut-eye at night, and you wake up to a few limbering exercises in the morning. It was all a matter of schedule. How to allot time in the morning for a few phone calls and greetings and shopping in the afternoons. With a few bucks to spare, she could buy things all throughout the corridor of shops and still have change to spend at the hairdresser. She would never have these luxuries if she stayed where she came from.

Michael put on his sneakers and tied his shoelaces. He headed out the door and into the park with his pregnant wife. He unfolded a big gray blanket on the grass and lied down facing the scorching sun. He would look at the squirrels scurrying among the branches of the giant oak trees. He could smell the grass and the yellow flowers of wayward weeds and thought to himself how lucky he was to live in a land of unpredictable weather. It was raining one night, and now the sun was shining in full force drying the camp grounds and the shrubs nearby.

Anita handed him a tuna sandwich with tomatoes from a small picnic basket which he ate heartily. The morning was pleasant so far with only a few passersby walking their dogs. There were no flies that would pester them, only a handful of yellow butterflies that pollinated the flowers nearby. It was an idyllic setting for a family that settled at the center of the city. The buzz of a lawnmower trimming the grass was heard not far off. Beyond them was the mountain that bore trees with leaves of changing color. The leaves had the autumn flair with colors ranging from yellow to orange to fiery red. It was still warm with southerly winds that was losing its grip due to an advancing autumn. The changing of the seasons was a sight to behold and its effect on the landscape.

Each season had its distinct brush stroke leaving its mark on the trees, on the bushes, and on the density of the air. Anita gave him a bottle of water which he drank lustily to quench his thirst from the noonday sun. It was a picture-perfect day at the park just lying lazily on the grass and a blank state of mind.

The wedding of Gerald and Ava came through without delay. The event was beamed live on TV aired by WTN, a major news network. Foreign dignitaries and government officials had been invited while the curious onlookers lined the streets. The traffic had been rerouted to pave the way for a retinue of cars, limousines, SUVs, and of course, the carriage which Ava rode to the cathedral. The British ambassador remarked that it was like a royal wedding with the bride wearing a tiara in her hair and rode a horse-drawn gilded carriage.

After a few minutes passing a tree-line boulevard, the bride finally alighted from the carriage and walked the steps of the cathedral without an escort. Her brother Michael met her at the door which she jauntily entered and into the massive cathedral. There were bugle horns that played, and a page announced the entrance of the bride. She strode along the aisle with a thin white veil covering her face. Her groom was waiting for her near the altar dressed like a man from the cavalry brigade with a sword hanging to the right side. As the couple knelt before the priest, he sprinkled holy water on them and released a pair of doves in the air. They exchanged vows and traded rings, a diamond ring for the bride and a gold ring for the groom.

After the wedding had been consummated, the priest said it was time for the groom to kiss the bride. After this took place, the crowd burst into wild applause. After the rites were concluded, the married couple walked down the aisle toward the door greeting well-wishers. They rode the carriage together and proceeded to a rented villa not far from the cathedral where they fed and entertained guests throughout the evening.

Three months after the wedding, Ava tested positive for pregnancy. She went to her obstetrician to do some ultrasound, and it revealed that the baby she was carrying was a boy. She could hardly contain herself and relayed the information to Gerald's secretary, Kathryn Cleaver. Ava said she was delighted to carry Gerald's baby and fulfilled the prediction that it would be a wanted child. Ava would accomplish her husband's request that she bring forth an heir thereby handing down the name to the next generation for posterity's sake. The unfortunate incident during her earlier marriage did not diminish her propensity for child bearing. She preferred not to talk about it. She was a physically fit PM, and her pregnancy would not be affected by some abnormality or damage to her uterus. She could give birth to as many children as she desired. She had no doubts in her mind that maternity would be richly rewarding. She was in the company of a rich man who answered her every need, and now she was going to reciprocate that with what he wanted most, a son. No other creature could ever fulfill that role besides a woman. The crown jewels lay in her womb waiting to be fertilized and brought to this world through the flesh. She alone had the legitimate authority to bear children for her husband since their juncture was solemnized by the church.

If her husband had affairs with other women, their offspring would be bastards not liable to inherit his vast fortune. They would be at the outer fringes of society with no legal right to carry the name. Ava basked in the limelight as the wife of a government official and who commanded respect and recognition from her peers. She was on the cover of glossy magazines and newsprint speaking about her role as the feminine touch behind the throne of her husband. She toured her Scarborough riding as if it was her playground, inspecting parks and taking away litter, walking down sidewalks to see if there was any obstruction, and taking a glance at the river to make sure that they were rid of toxic waste. She reveled in her official function as the prima donna of her riding.

She instilled discipline and fortitude to her workers and staff that they may do their work with speed and efficiency. She spared no one who was found fault with laziness or a dereliction of duties. Their life at home was filled with love and understanding. They rarely had spats, and every day they would greet each other with words like honey or sweetheart. Every morning, Ava would carry a tray of toast, omelette, and juice. Gerald had breakfast in bed if he wasn't in a hurry. They had a maid who would iron Gerald's shirts and pants and clean the house once it was empty. A cook prepared the meals under Ava's supervision. The cook served a wide variety of food including steak tartar, beef stroganoff, lamb chops with garlic, roast chicken with potatoes, and a lot of more. Gerald usually ate dinner at home after a busy day at the office. They had a washing machine and a dryer so the laundry was conveniently done at home. As for the suits, Ava sent them to the dry cleaner. In anticipation for the big day when the baby will finally be born, Ava bought a crib and painted the baby's room blue. She bought toys, teddy bears, and children's books of nursery rhymes. The room had a wall-to-wall carpet and a video camera so that Ava would know what was going on. There was round-the- clock surveillance so that there would be no chance of a mishap or accident. She hired a nanny who was highly recommended by the agency and told her to stand by for the big day. The nanny's references were excellent, and she was well-trained for the job. No criminal record with an impressive work history.

With the help of a nanny, Ava could accompany her husband to trips around the country and abroad. She would stand beside her husband shaking hands with illustrious visitors and pour tea in the well-decorated office. Ava was a good hostess, modeling clothes from local fashion designers like Makropoulos, Schiaparelli, and Scandini, with composure and the requisite statuesque pose.

Then one day, the television crew from the WTN network came to her residence to conduct an interview. Ava spoke with the popular TV host, Cindy Adams, who did a one-on-one interview. Ava wore a fuchsia pink dress that reached her knees with matching shoes.

Cindy Adams: How big of an influence are you with your husband?

Ava Dalton: Not significant. I just make sure that the bylaws passed by the council are enforced. Like no dog litter on the parks, no pit bulls or other dangerous dogs on the prowl so nobody gets hurt, the shrubs are trimmed while the falling leaves are raked and disposed of. I also make sure that there are no obstructions to power lines. I call hydro for any fallen transmitters due to natural calamities. I also see to it that the streets are well lit, replacing lightbulbs that have lost their brightness.

Cindy Adams: I notice a change in the appearance of your husband. Do you have anything to do with this?

Ava Dalton: Whereas before he didn't have anyone to attend to his clothes, I now pick the suits and ties he wears to different occasions. I make sure he gets regular exercise whenever he has the time on our private gym. And for his hair, I bring him to a hair salon so he can color the grays on his head and have a nice haircut.

Cindy Adams: You're expecting your first child. Has the mood changed in your household?

Ava Dalton: It's all very uplifting. Gerald is very excited about the baby. He was praying for this day to come. He's lined up a list of godparents but can't seem to agree on the name of the baby. It's his first time to be a father, so I think he's a bit nervous. All in all, we're upbeat, and there's so much preparation going on inside the house. Cindy Adams: Do you have any misgivings about marrying your husband since he's a very busy man and might not have enough time for the family?

Ava Dalton: On the contrary, he comes home every night to me, and we talk about the events of the day.

I visit him in the office quite often, and he takes me to his trips out of town. I get all the attention I want, and there has never been a dull moment. We're a team, and I give him input on the crucial decisions he's about to make. I am not your ordinary housewife who will sulk in one corner while he plays golf with his associates. I am an active participant in his reign over our riding. I am not going to stay in the background while he rubs elbows with the rich and the mighty. He will take me along with him so that I can learn the ropes of his profession.

We are in this together like two peas in a pod.

Cindy Adams: You're an upstart in the world of politics because you married your husband only three months ago. How has the change affected you?

Ava Dalton: I am relishing every minute of it. My schedule has been so regimented that I now not only deal with the trivial issues but also the more crucial ones. Being an elected official's wile is a twenty-four-hour job that requires a lot of effort in maintaining a lot of balance at home and in the riding. I make sure that questions in council meetings are heard and answered.

Our constituents can run to me, and I will direct them to the proper channels.

Cindy Adams: In your hectic schedule, you're bound to miss a step or two. How have you managed to put on such a calm demeanor? Ava Dalton: I may look calm on the outside, but I'm already fidgeting about booking his appointments. I know it is his secretary's job, but I also help in easing the transition from home buddy to government official. It's not a joke being summoned to the office for an important cabinet meeting. In the morning, I'm all nerves because of the barrage of phone calls. I take down messages and relay them to my husband. He promises to get back to those messages and answer them. Maybe not right away but as soon as the busy schedule subsides. I am up to my neck doing errands for my husband. Luckily, we have an efficient staff who takes care of those things.

Cindy Adams: There's been an attempt on the lives of some foreign leaders. Do you make sure your husband is out of danger? Ava Dalton: The details of security are with the provincial government. He has several bodyguards following him everywhere he goes. Several hateful messages posted on line have been dealt with by security. Other than that, my husband doesn't have any problems roaming the country or giving speeches in town hall meetings. He is well loved by his constituents, and his outreach to voters keeps growing.

Cindy Adams: As the wife of a legislator, you have a duty to keep the motor running. What happens when fatigue sets in?

Ava Dalton: Me and my husband have boundless energy. He was elected to serve the riding of Scarborough, and in that capacity, he has sworn his tireless pursuits to protect the rights of citizens. He has adequate sleep and weekends off unless there is a ribbon cutting event that requires his presence. He is still young and has extensive experience as an MP. That means he'll devote many more years of his life to public service.

Six months later, Ava gave birth to a bouncing baby boy. Gerald welcomed the newest addition to the family with glee and outright joy. He couldn't think of a better gift for his otherwise solitary and worthless life.

Now he'd have someone to cuddle with and sing tunes to. Straight from work, he'd be beside the crib contemplating on their future together, watching him crawl on all fours. He'd learn to feed him with baby food and change the diapers. When the baby would cry at night, he'd get up and cradle him in his arms. If the baby would get a little fever, Gerald would take time off from the office and bring him to the pediatrician. He knew that the baby would be vulnerable to diseases which is why he made sure that the baby was immunized and vaccinated. It was his first time to be a father, and he took the role seriously. With a video camera, he recorded the first steps of the child and the touching moments with his mother. On the child's first birthday, he hired a troupe of clowns accompanied by Chihuahuas who did tricks for the scores of children who attended. It was an unforgettable stage in his life as he watched the child grow and mumble his first words.

Two years later, the provincial elections in Quebec was well underway. The Independence Party fielded candidates in every circumscription. Monique Bovette, along with Jerome Leblanc, the chief party strategist, was in the forefront of a long, arduous campaign. They tried to convince voters that independence was the only way to regain their lost identity. The erosion of the French language was attributed to the fact that English was making headway in elementary and high schools. Quebec needed to restrict the introduction of English subjects into the curriculum. In doing so, the Quebec government would have to hire and train French teachers so that the students would master the French language. Another reason for independence was for the rise inprominence of the Quebec foreign delegation. As it is, Quebec is represented by federal personnel who display the Canadian flag. Even the premier of Quebec has the maple leaf flag draped in the background. The has to change, argued Monique Bovette. In conferences abroad, Quebec should be represented by the fleur- de-lis flag as it is only fitting that an autonomous province should opt for its own insignia and colors.

The Independence Party let it be known that they would hold a referendum on the first mandate. The time for independence is now because things were getting out of hand. The francophone population was complaining that the influx of English-speaking immigrants were diluting their identity. They did not wish to assimilate to the Quebecois population which is the reason why French instruction was declining. Monique Bovette proposed strict border controls to ward off undesirable aliens who do not fit the ideal profile. Only when Quebec can screen newcomers for unwanted characteristics can it truly be independent.

The Quebec foreign office is encouraging immigration from France and other French-speaking countries. An independent Quebec would do this job more efficiently since they will be able to conduct interviews in French and glean from their work experience which candidates truly fit outstanding qualifications. As it is now, the Quebec foreign delegation operates under the shadow of the Canadian embassy and cannot effectively perform consular duties to their own specifications.

The Independence Party faced weak opposition from the struggling Liberal Party. The Liberal Party was so disorganized and loosely knit that it failed to deliver on its promises. First there was a question of government funding.

Bombardier, a manufacturer of planes and trains, had to lay off thousands of workers due to a slash in government funding. Healthcare workers walked out of their jobs due to a freeze on their salaries not taking into consideration the high rate of inflation. Public museums had to shorten their hours of operation due to the unavailability of government funds. And projects of the performing arts and artists had to be shelved due to a lack of government subsidy.

It was a very bad year for the economy that registered in the negative figures. The Quebec economic sector depends a lot on government financing. And when the flow of cash is staunched, then a myriad of companies and services feel the crunch. The welfare office even had to suspend check remittances to a lot of recipients due to irregular government support. The Independence Party promised to rectify the situation by increasing exports to Europe and drawing up a free trade agreement with France thereby increasing cash flow.

Another area where the Liberals failed miserably is the legalization of marijuana. Many Quebecois parents felt that this measure was untimely and disastrous for their children. They were convinced that pot could lead to impaired driving, lower scholastic abilities, and alteration of the functions of the brain. If they had it their way, they would ban the drug and send those who sell it to jail. They wanted their children to excel in school and aim high in their chosen fields. Marijuana would lower their propensity for academic excellence and hamper their rise in society.

It has been proven that marijuana contributes to the rise of criminal activity. The steep price of the drug forces adolescents to steal just so they can afford to support the habit. While Quebec is waging a vigorous campaign against cigarette smoking, it shouldn't pave the way for consumption of yet a more dangerous drug. The smoke from marijuana contains many toxic substances that are harmful to one's health. The consumption of brownies and other edible food laced with marijuana could lead to delirium and insanity. Quebec parents have the right to protect their children from harmful products, and that means we have to rescind this law.

Another reason for the decline of the popularity of the reigning Liberal Party was the skyrocketing price of gasoline at the pump. Either the oil wells in Alberta was drying up or they just weren't drilling enough oil to satiate the demands of other provinces. The manufacture of oil in Newfoundland wasn't operational yet, and there were few other places where they could do oil exploration. The subterranean floor of the Arctic ocean was the last place they could go because they didn't want to interfere with the pristine nature of the virgin territory. And the choice of the railway as a means to transport combustible fuel was highly questionable, especially after the Lac Megantic disaster that cost the lives of many inhabitants. Add to that, the oil spill at the St. Laurent river destroyed much of the ecosystem in the area, and the projected cleanup could take years.

The Independence Party would insist on more seaworthy vessels and upon closer inspection that the hulls of ships and barges would have no leaks or ruptures. The oil from Alberta would be transported by pipelines so that there would be minimal damage to the environment.

The poor record of the Liberal Party didn't pass muster during the televised debates. All they could do was stutter and mutter inanities that made no sense. Upon cross-examination, the Liberal Party chief could not come up with one achievement in the domain of the economy. He was caught red-handed when asked about his projects for the accomplishment of such a proposal. They were bereft of any valid prospects that would meet the demands of the economy.

On the other hand, the Independence Party showed a comprehensive study on what they would do once they gain power. They would ask the Alberta oil companies to sell fuel at a fraction of the cost since they will have to pay tariffs and duties for their export. Quebec would export their hydroelectric power to the provinces of Canada, thereby collecting much-needed revenue. Quebec would build dams in the northern part of the province, thereby creating hydroelectric power that will meet the energy demands of the province. Quebec would export lumber and food products to France to take advantage of lower tariffs due to the free trade agreement and closer cooperation.

It was election day, and there was a high turnout of voters. There was confusion at the polling stations since many eligible voters couldn't find their names on the voters list. It was a hectic Wednesday when voters waited a long time lining up just to vote. There were emergency crews handing out cool refreshments to voters who grew weary waiting in the blistering sun. Then as sunset approached and all the voters had already cast their ballot, the polling stations closed and began the tedious job of counting the votes. The votes were in, and the counting was tabulated by a prestigious accounting firm.

By ten o'clock in the evening, various newscast carried the preliminary results showing the Independence Party candidates leading the pack. It wasn't surprising at all since many were swayed by the fiery speeches of Monique Bovette and Jerome Leblanc. It was a marathon telecast which by midnight showed that the majority of Independence Party candidates were elected into office. At the headquarters of the Independence Party, a perfectly coiffed Monique Bovette wearing a blue dress with matching sapphire earrings went to the podium and thanked their supporters for a stunning landslide victory.

The crippled Liberal Party would no longer stand in the way of a third referendum when the Quebec population would be asked whether they wanted independence for their province. As recent surveys have shown, the majority of the Quebec population wanted to break free from Canada and form a closer alliance with France. It would be the accomplishment of the self-fulfilling prophecy of the late lamented Frenchman Charles de Gaulle when he stated in the balcony, "Long live the free Quebec."

The Quebecois population have had it with the federal government who ran short on their promises: Quebec was a big province endowed with many natural resources that could sustain a high standard of living. There were none who were living below the poverty line, and jobs were aplenty as long as you could speak French.

Now that the separatists were in power, the order of the day was to strengthen Bill 101 which sought to promote the French language in every nook and cranny in the province. This meant no English signs on commercial establishments with the French language prominently displayed. This meant that employees had to speak French to their customers to fulfill the letter of the law. Any employee who was lacking in French language skills would be booted out of the company or be directed to a French immersion program. It was all in keeping with the government's incentive to put French first. A lot of stores were contemplating on moving to Ontario due to the severity of the language laws. But the government offered free French lessons to neophytes who had just settled in Quebec. Therefore there was no excuse in not knowing how to speak French.

A cornerstone of the separatist government was to tighten the control of greenhouse gas emissions. The Quebec government would send a delegation to the climate change conference in Paris to sign the accord that would limit air pollution to a minimum level. Monique Bovette was very much concerned over the nefarious effects of exhaust fumes from cars and trucks and the smog generated by factories. The melting of the ice caps in the north pole and the unusually warm weather in the northern part of the province were all signs of the deterioration of the climate that were caused by human activity. The frequent occurrence of tornados and strong winds as well as the flooding of low lying areas that were close to rivers are all a symptom of a change of weather pattern. So much heat trapped in the atmosphere that it elicits unexpected bursts of moisture that fall down in the form of rain. Many towns had to be evacuated due to the overflowing of rivers. Through the concerted effort of the National Guard and the fire department, sandbags were put in place to stop the inordinate flow of water into homes.

A project of the recently elected government is the extension of the subway system in Montreal. A lot of passengers have been griping about the slow service of buses. To compensate for the lack of buses, the government has laid out plans to extend the blue line so that commuters can get to their destination faster. A lot of areas in Montreal don't have access to subway service. The government is willing to change that.

They are cognizant of the fact that with a more efficient subway system comprising of many more stations, the city's traffic situation will be improved. It is the government's incentive to passengers to leave their cars at home.

It was at the conference of Liberal Party members in Ontario when Gerald Dalton, the MP for Scarborough, made rabid pronouncements against the Independence Party of Quebec. He said that Monique Bovette, the apparent leader of the Independence Party, was out to wreck and divide the nation. It was very devious of her to entice the province into voting for separation by pointing to the shortcomings of the federal government when, as a matter of fact, Quebec was faring better inside the confederation than at any point in its history. If Quebec would secede from Canada that would give rise to the far right political parties which would carry out ethnic cleansing. Massive deportations of nonwhite people would take place due to the unbridled nationalistic fervor gripping the province. His advice to the inhabitants of Quebec was to take it easy on nonfrancophone immigrants and to give them a chance to integrate.

Canada is a wonderful country where newcomers from the four corners of the world mix and match. They bring with them a diversity of cultures and languages that enrich and embellish the social fabric of the nation.

It is bad to have one dominant culture rule over the rest. The country is a babble of tongues built on the foundation of democratic values. Freedom of expression is granted to everyone, and people are free to practice their faith. It is not like Quebec where you cannot display signs in the language of your choice. You can build mosques, temples, and pagodas where you will be left to the serenity of the environment.

Canada is a safe haven for people fleeing religious persecution, famine, and wars. Refugees from the Middle East, Africa, and Asia have all successfully built new lives who at one point started from scratch. Their thriving communities are a testament to the country's healthy economy.

Gerald Dalton was appealing to Quebecois voters to reject separation and instead hold on to Canadian unity and reaffirm their faith in the multicultural character of the country. He cited the myopic vision of Quebec's governing party as a stumbling block to the expansion of local industries. Progress can only come if there is a diversification in the means of livelihood and a tolerance of the cultural differences of workers. Salaries should be commensurate to the qualifications of workers and not hinge on superfluous demands like language skills. Diplomas obtained from overseas should be given equivalent status in the province to offset the shortage of doctors, nurses, and engineers. There is a backlog in immigrant applications due to the province's stance in handing out residence certificates. Unless this is corrected, the province won't meet its quota for immigration.

The cutback in the granting of visas to temporary workers is putting a strain in the agricultural sector.

Many laborers are being deprived of heath care privileges due to the tendency of some landowners to hire under the table. There are nongovernmental agencies which are fighting for the rights of undocumented workers so that they are protected by the law. Many workers, some from as far away as Guatemala, are being paid a pittance of their salary due to their irregular status. The government should rectify this injustice by offering residency to these migrant workers and compensating their lack of status.

Canada is a rich and generous country that rewards deserving workers the rights to residency and other perks as part of a salary package. It only hopes that Quebec does its share.

High immigration levels is a measure undertaken by the government to offset the declining birth rate among Canadian women. Many Canadian women are postponing motherhood so that they can pursue higher learning and to attain higher positions in their field of employment. The government is at a quandary as to how it can replenish its ageing workforce. With the entry of foreign labor, the country can solve the shortage of workers.

English classes are available to immigrants who have a poor grasp of the English language. Interpreters from various cultural communities such as Punjab, Chinese, and Arabic are on standby mode to ensure the fluid transition and integration of workers. The abundance of resources cannot be underestimated since these programs will be available to workers who get laid off or are simply unemployed. Seasonal workers, for instance, can collect unemployment benefits simply by filling out forms and providing the agency with their discharge certificates. Once the forms are collated and processed, laid-off workers can now begin to receive their checks by mail or through direct deposit. This is a system of payments that has earned the country a reputation for fairness.

Another question posed by Gerald Dalton is Quebec's inability to fight terrorism. Only Canada has the capability to sift through information gathered by its intelligence agencies. Every four years, the government collects data from its residents through a nationwide census. The information then is fed to its database where questions of ethnicity, language, and employment are stored. This provides the authorities with an accurate profile of its inhabitants. The information gives the government a detailed assessment of the tendencies, cultural norms, and programs of the services it will dish out to the population.

It also gives the government the ability to gauge the cross-section of the population with its propensity toward violence, conflict, and strife. Measures will be taken to deter the incidence of violence and to ensure the convivial atmosphere of communities.

The Royal Canadian Mounted Police has a wide-ranging estimation of the proclivities of cultural communities toward the disruption of peace and tranquility. These pockets of hostility groups are constantly being monitored so that they pose no danger to the general public. If there is any sign of a resumption of violence, the RCMP will act on it immediately.

Due to the political uncertainty in Quebec, Michael Collins, his wife, Anita, and their two kids headed to Toronto, Ontario. There they would raise a family in a more congenial atmosphere and belonging to a multilingual society. They know that their right to freedom of expression would be curtailed due to the strict language laws. They wanted to infuse a more broadminded way of thinking to their children who won't be coerced into speaking a language with a harsh set of laws. They believed that the more languages you could speak will open up opportunities for growth and development.

But Anita had some misgivings about moving to Ontario. She was perfectly at ease with French since she grew up speaking Creole which was strongly influenced by French. But then she knew that English was the lingua franca of the world, and this meant a lot for the future of her children. All the modern inventions and terminologies were being developed by the Americans, and it would be advantageous if their children were familiar with the American mind-set. That is why she agreed into moving to Ontario.

Another thing that Anita would miss about Montreal are the leisurely rides they took on horse-drawn caleches. They would ride past old buildings in old Montreal amid the summer heat. They liked the sound of the hooves hitting the cobbled pavement, and the driver maneuver the reins so that the horse would walk on a straight line. She would wear a wide-brimmed hat with sunglasses as she imbibed the scents of wild flowers undulating in the wind. She would also miss the winding staircases that decorate the facades of the homes in Montreal. Many postcards feature this scenery, and she sends them to her relatives in the Caribbean so they can appreciate and have a glimpse into Montreal architecture. She lives in a home with a spiral staircase, and she's grown used to climbing it every day. She likes to go up and down the staircase as a snake slithers in the branches of a tree. But now she has to say goodbye to it and instead live in a building with a lobby entrance. She will miss the charm and old-fashioned character of Montreal with all its quaint architecture and the French joy of living.

It was at about this time that the mother of Michael and Ava died. She fought a long and arduous battle with brain cancer to which she eventually succumbed. She took an assortment of pills and underwent CT scan but to no avail. There was nothing the neurologists and oncologists could do to hamper the spread of cancer. The malignant cells spread throughout her entire body that proved debilitating and turned her into a vegetative state.

Only Ava was at her bedside supervising the installation of a feeding tube and intravenous ducts. She left all of her wealth to Ava which was substantial for having married into aristocracy. She tried to bridge the gap between her mother and her brother, Michael, but she was obstinate in not having anything to do with him. As far as the mother was concerned, Michael was an outcast who chose to live with the scum of the earth. It's a pity that the mother chose to disown one of her two kids and not enjoy the company of her grandchildren. If she had only opened her eyes to the diversity of people around her and observed the transmission of her genetic material to her grandkids.

Michael did not attend the funeral of his mother for reasons that are well-known to the reader. Instead Michael brought his wife and kids on top of the CN tower to enjoy the view of the city. Ava, for her part, wrote an obituary about her mother in the newspaper. In it she narrated the kind of illness the mother suffered and thanked everyone who shared in the last moments of her life.

Michael did not suffer mental trauma due to his irreconcilable differences with his mother. He blocked all incoming information from his wife whom he doted upon and nurtured a fruitful relationship. As far as Michael was concerned, his family was foremost in his list of priorities. He had an amiable relationship with his sister with whom he shared his anxieties about the future. They both were in Ontario now, far from the skirmishes in Quebec. They would call each other up, relaying tidbits of information. While Ava was dressed in black mourning over the loss of her mother, Michael was upbeat about his new environment. Michael didn't show a tinge of despair over the recent events but was optimistic due to the polyglot character of the province. There were Chinese merchants, Indian shopkeepers, and Filipino nannies who all lent a distinctive cosmopolitan ambiance to the city. Toronto was a bustling metropolis with street sales and parades happening almost simultaneously. There was the parade of Caribbean nations whose partygoers wore skimpy outfits to the tune of metallic drums. Not to be missed was the gay parade with participants in drag costumes and bare breasted attires. The prime minister and other officials partook of the festivities marching alongside the revelers.

Michael was content to be in Ontario. It was a far cry from the bland character in Quebec. Here he saw signs in Chinese and Punjabi adorning commercial establishments. The boulevards were wider the better to accommodate trams and cars. He would bring his kids to Marineland so they could enjoy the rides and see wild animals in their natural habitat. And most of all to see the Niagara Falls with its roaring waters cascading down to the lake. All the wonders of nature are here. All you have to do is to book yourself on a tour bus that will bring you to awesome destinations. Ontario has an efficient mass transit system, and you can go places with ease.

After the conference, Gerald Dalton went down the stage to shake hands with well-wishers and Liberal Party members. A marching music was blaring from the loudspeakers as the audience went into rapturous applause. Some were holding onto red balloons; still others were holding placards that sent a message of unity across this vast country. Then several minutes later, a man in a gray suit darted from the back, and instead of shaking the hand, he pulled out a revolver and shot Gerald Dalton, the MP from Scarborough, at close range. Three shots rang out, and Gerald fell on the floor with blood splattered on his shirt.

Immediately, security personnel tackled the man and wrestled him on the floor. He was handcuffed and taken away. Gerald Dalton was rushed to a waiting ambulance, and it sped with sirens in the direction of the hospital. He was pronounced dead on arrival, and news of his death was flashed on all TV channels. It was breaking news, and the identity of the assailant was carried on the early evening news. Ava heard the news on TV and was completely devastated by the announcement. The phone rang, and it was the police who asked her to come to the morgue and claim the body.

The name of the assassin was Frederic Duclos who was a sympathizer of the separatist movement in Quebec. He deliberately travelled to Ontario to stop Gerald Dalton from spewing out vitriolic messages that would hinder the Yes campaign of the Independence Party. Monique Bovette distanced herself from the assassin saying that she did not know the man and that nobody instructed him to do it. She also added that no one could stop the Yes campaign from gaining momentum. Frederic Duclos was arraigned later in the week and was detained in the penitentiary pending a swift and judicious trial. There were many witnesses who saw Mr. Duclos pull out a gun. It was even captured in videotape, so there was incontrovertible proof of the culpability of Mr. Duclos.

Upon interrogation at the police precinct, Mr. Duclos tried to divert the attention to the fact that Quebec needed to be an independent country so it could exercise its freedom to choose which path to take. Gerald Dalton was an obstacle to the road to independence and had to be eliminated. Mr. Duclos invoked his right to a lawyer and a speedy trial saying he would give no further statements for fear of incriminating himself.

The prime minister of Canada and other high-ranking government officials, as well as several premiers of provinces, attended the funeral ceremonies of Gerald Dalton. The cortege bearing the body of the deceased drove from the palatial home of Ava into the grounds of St. John the Baptist church in Scarborough. Ava was accompanied by her five-year-old son, Brian, and Michael's family. They were all dressed in black with Ava wearing a see-through black veil. The first to deliver a eulogy was the prime minister of Canada. He spoke thus.

"Today we mourn the passing of a great public servant whose service to the government was exemplary and outstanding. A great man was taken away from us through a hail of gunfire by a deranged criminal. The senseless act of violence has once again marred the picturesque beauty of our tranquil province. We will not cower in fear and give into intimidation by ruthless fanatics. We must be strong and stand upright in the face of adversity and gather our forces so that we can deliver the goods to our constituents. We must not shrink from our goals just because there is conflict from the enemies of the state. We shall have a firm resolve to do our job as best we can even if it means going the extra mile to provide security for our elected officials.

"Under the administration of Gerald Dalton, the economy of the province of Ontario grew by leaps and bounds. The spending budget of the province now stands at a whopping hundred billion dollars. He made those factories working again. He started those car plants rolling again with new models. He injected new capital to the manufacturing firms including pharmaceuticals and clothing businesses. He fixed roads and built bridges. He improved the infrastructure of the province and constructed superhospitals that cater to the sick at no cost. Not once was he accused of misappropriation of funds. He was an honest man who had the talent for doing wise investments. He promoted the healthy business climate of the province wooing investors from here and abroad. Ontario is a first-rate province, thanks to his savvy business deals. Under his leadership, food banks were able to accumulate a vast number of goods. No more should the needy go empty-handed while warehouses are well stocked with canned food and nonperishable items. We've lost a man of great stature and a friend to the rich and poor alike."

It was Ava's turn to talk. She lifted her sunglasses, and the bags under her eyes were exposed. Either due to lack of sleep or constant crying. She adjusted the microphone and nervously spoke.

"A week ago, my husband was taken away from me by an overzealous separatist who opposed my husband's point of view. All my husband was doing was for the good of the country. He was vehemently against the separation of Quebec since both sides shared a common history, values, and goals. My husband worked tirelessly for the upliftment of the economy of Quebec, making last-minute pleas to the directorate so they would form a more cohesive unit with the rest of Canada. But that was not the case. "The only man who could integrate Quebec to the confederation was shot to death by an act of deliberate murder. I cry myself to sleep at night worrying that my only son will not know who his father was. Yet my husband's legacy moves on in the industries he helped create and in the infrastructure he built. You can never put down a man who has invested so much time and effort developing the economy of a nation to what it is now. He was a man who was determined to rid the province of corruption and send to jail the erring officials who were guilty of accepting kickbacks and bribes. "Regardless of his father's untimely demise, I hope my son follows in his footsteps and seeks to serve the general public when the time comes. In this moment of sorrow, I implore the public to demand justice so that the culprit suffers the punishment for the heinous act he has committed. He has mortally wounded our family and deprived Ontario of a very studious planner. A voice for equality and freedom has been lost all because of a gun toting hoodlum. We need a total ban on firearms to keep the peace and tranquility of our streets and neighborhood.

"I never thought I'd become a widow at such an early age, bereft of a man who promised me love and happiness all the days of my life. We need to protect our freedom of speech so that no crazed gunman shatters our existence. It is our right to speak out against the ills of society so that they don't threaten our way of life. I am retiring from public life and seek to return to the confines of a private citizen. I will keep a watchful eye on current events and provincial matters. I will seek the maximum penalty for people who commit serious crimes."

A year after they were sworn into office, the separatist government of Quebec held a referendum on Quebec sovereignty. The question couldn't be clearer: Are you in favor of the separation of Quebec from the rest of Canada and become an independent country? It was a balmy day in October when hordes of voters formed long queues outside polling stations just to cast a ballot in this historic occasion. Monique Bovette and chief party strategist, Jerome Leblanc, led a long and hard campaign just so that the French-speaking population come out in full force to support the affirmative vote. The polling booths were open from 8:00 am to 8:00 pm.

Many office workers, teachers, and laborers were given the afternoon off just so they could vote. By 10:00 pm, the evening newscasts were reporting preliminary results of the referendum. It wouldn't be until midnight when the bulk of results were reported in to show an irreversible lead of whichever vote. Monique Bovette fended off rumors that there would be a power struggle once Quebec becomes independent. It was widely known that Monique Bovette was at the forefront to becoming Quebec's head of state. They would ditch the queen and become a republic from the same mold as France.

The following day, all newspapers reported about the stunning victory of the Yes campaign. Quebec was on the road to becoming a sovereign country. The president of France issued a statement congratulating the Quebecois people for their hard-won struggle toward independence. The time is now ripe for creating closer ties and an economic bloc between the two countries. Preserving the French language is at the top of the agenda. The free movement of citizens and goods is being studied. There will be a closer cooperation, and security information is to be shared on both sides of the Atlantic. There is going to be vigorous cultural exchange so that each country becomes a showcase of a rich heritage of traditions. They will beef up security so that there will be no terrorist threats and danger to the public. Quebec will adopt the euro as its official currency so that there will be uniformity in the value of transactions. Airbus will set up a subsidiary in Quebec to provide jobs to thousands of Quebecers. French professionals will travel to Quebec to help train engineers, doctors, and mechanics. It is one step to put Quebec on its feet so that it can face the challenges of tomorrow. Quebec has the talent and resources to be on par with France.

The prime minister went on a televised address which was beamed all across Canada. This is his speech:

We are a smaller country now that Quebec has decided to separate. But our country still straddles the three oceans: the Pacific, the Atlantic and the Arctic. Our country will still be a leader of many industries since the economy is well developed. Our strength in the global stage has not diminished and we will still be a valuable member of world organizations. Although our country has been divided, we are still united by our push for multiculturalism and integration of ethnic communities. Now that our French-speaking neighbors, have decided to go their own way, we are more than ever a bastion of English-speaking people who swear allegiance to the British monarchy. We are still as big as Australia, and we will cultivate close relations with the United Kingdom. Our airports, sea lanes, lakes, and rivers are all equipped with modern transport facilities which will make movement between remote towns and major cities to be easier. Telecommunication and electric power lines crisscross the vast north which makes interaction between people faster and more efficient. We are united by our pursuit of happiness, the maintenance of a high standard of living, and the growth of our oil industry.

In the Independence Party headquarters Monique Bovette took center stage to deliver a key note address. She was greeted with cheers from all corners of the auditorium.

"At last, we are a country. We have at last claimed our destiny which is to carry the torch of the French language and culture in North America. Immediately, our government officials will strengthen our relations with France and open up the widest possible avenues of cooperation. The road to Ontario is open to those people who disagree with our goals and values. But it is a one-way ticket, and the prospects of returning to Quebec is not good. We will militarize our borders, and those not having Quebec papers like a driver's license, a Quebec birth certificate, or a Quebec Medicare card will not be allowed to enter.

"We will compile a census in the territory so that each inhabitant will be duly registered. Services to the public will only be done in French so we will be able to count the number of beds in the hospitals and ascertain that they go to the citizen of this new country. We will form a military to better defend our territory from outsiders who want to filch our wealth. And lastly, we will make sure that our fleur-de-lis flag flies proudly in our legislature and government buildings."

The mood was one of optimism in the streets of Montreal following the success of the referendum. People were chattering in French saying how fortunate they were to be an ally and close cousin of France. They packed cafés and open air terraces hugging one another. Cheerful of the fact that got rid of the shadow that relegated them to subordination. They were free from the yoke of oppression and were now poised to do business in French with the rest of the world. Many waved the flag of Quebec and painted their cheeks with the blue fleur-de-lis.

The euphoria lasted for over a month when fireworks were launched from the Champlain bridge radiating brilliant colors. Air force jets flew in the clear sky leaving a trail of smoke in many colors. The bells in St. Joseph oratory rang loudly to celebrate the birth of a nation. The mayor of Montreal gave the keys of the city to the famous painter, Jean Dagenais, for depicting the landscape of Quebec in his paintings. One of his canvases would be exhibited prominently at the city hall. Quebec would send its own team to the Olympic games, thereby showcasing the talent and stamina of its own athletes. Quebec would also send its own candidates to beauty pageants thereby hoisting the Quebec flag.

One person who did not share in the festivities of the general population was Susan Downer, the Concordia professor who made a brief cameo appearance at the restaurant. She knew her rights would be trampled upon and that it would be no use to carp about the denial of English services since the present government made it clear in a communiqué that all communication would be done in French. Her only option was to move to Ontario so she could continue holding a Canadian passport. She was greatly disappointed by the referendum results citing the poor coordination of the federal government in enticing the voters to say no to separation. She would have to uproot herself from her neighborhood and establish new contacts in another province. She would have to start from scratch and see the light in a new horizon.

She was averse to waving the Quebec flag and even after all these years still had difficulty comprehending the French language. Her leaving Quebec was like a deportation order. She couldn't bear being cut off from Canada and being denied the right to speak in English. She'd probably hitch a ride with a friend who was also moving to Ontario and give Quebec one tearful last goodbye.

Ava was thinking about this for quite some time now ever since her husband was murdered. She would leave her son and her material assets behind to the care of her brother while she will go off and join an order of nuns. The Carmelite nuns had a convent, and she would inquire about their enclosure.

Her brother and his family would move into Ava's sprawling residence and manage her financial affairs. His wife would see to it that Brian would go to school every day and send him to bed in the evening. Meanwhile, Ava was met by the Mother Superior who wanted to ascertain whether Ava had the vocation for religious life. Only time will tell if Ava can follow the rigors of the life of an ascetic. She would have to get up at six in the morning to perform some daily ritual like saying prayers and getting together with the other nuns for a reflection on the gospel of the day. As part of her penance, she would have to scrub the bathroom floor with detergent and sweep the large bedroom where most nuns sleep. By midday she would have some lunch prepared by the cook of the convent who usually served the daily fare of chicken, soup, and bread. There were no alcoholic beverages in the convent.

Ava was summoned to the office of the Mother Superior who wanted to know why she joined the order of the nuns.

Ava explained, "Ever since my husband was assassinated, I felt this emptiness in my soul which I know can only be filled by the spirit of God. My life in the outside world is finished, and I have sought refuge in this place to say prayers with the other nuns. I have enjoyed the life of a high-society girl but found it to be unrewarding and devoid of any real significance. I expect to find peace and serenity within these walls, something which I have not found outside. I want to know exactly why my life turned upside down. Why I became a widow at so young an age and what plans does God have for me. Through the conversations and interactions with the other sisters, I may find an answer. But getting married for a third time is hardly the answer for me."

Then the Mother Superior asked her for how long she intended to stay in the convent.

Ava replied, "For as long as the wound hurts. My scars are still fresh, and they haven't healed. The time will come when there would be a new chance at life, but until then I can't see the sun shining in my direction."

The Mother Superior proceeded to question her, "The sisters tell me you have problems saying the rosary. We are a contemplative order which draws strength from saying prayers. When do you think you'll know how to say the rosary by heart?"

Ava replied with a faltering voice, "I'm only a novice who still has to get used to the life in the convent. Through repetition, I should be able to memorize saying the rosary. All I ask is that you be patient with me. As I stated before, I wasn't raised with a religious background, so all these rituals are new to me. I carry a booklet of prayers that spells out how to say the rosary.

"Whenever I get together with the rest of the sisters, I always bring it with me. Saying the rosary brings a spirit of tranquility. So I should learn it by memory."

The Mother Superior continued with her questions, "Sometimes I see you with your hair exposed to the elements. It is important to cover your hair with the habit to ward off peeping toms with prurient desires."

Ava answered, "The summer is just too unbearable. Sometimes sweat trickles down to my forehead and onto my cheeks. I need to unwrap my hair so I can get a breath of fresh air. But if the rule says I have to cover my hair to allay temptation, then I shall conform to it. I don't go out of the walls of the convent too often since all my needs are being met. But since there are members of the opposite sex that work in the convent, I have to be careful not to arouse unwanted attention."

The Mother Superior went on to question Ava, "I understand you have a son. What happens when he goes to look for you?"

Ava replied, "He's too young to understand what happened to his father. In due time, he'll realize that I needed to be sheltered from the outside world, away from the prying eyes of the public and the paparazzi to have a little privacy and seclusion. Everything I inherited from my husband will go to my son when he reaches legal age. For now, he's in the custody of my brother who attends to all his needs." The Mother Superior reiterated, "The doors of the convent are open for you to leave. We are not holding you against your will. If you have some unfinished business outside, then I that suggest that you attend to it."

Ava replied, "I greatly appreciate you accepting me into your convent. When the time comes for me to leave, I shall. All I ask is that you leave the doors open for me to come back."

Ava struck a friendship with one of the nuns. Her name was Sister Fidela, and she was of Hispanic origin. A tragedy in the family brought her to the confines of the Carmelite monastery. Law enforcement officers mistook her father as a member of a drug cartel and shot him the ensuing drug raid. Her mother got in the way and was also shot. Both the women would cry on each other's shoulders as they would recount the grim episodes of their lives.

Sometimes they would stroll in the garden picking flowers like marigolds, bougainvillea, and roses and place them on the altar.

The gardener would warn them not to pick too many flowers as some of the plants were just on the verge of growing buds. The gardener was a strong man using a hoe on the soil to make them ready for cultivation.

He gave Ava a wink to which she ignored. Ava was a holy woman now, and she would not entertain salacious advances. Ava and Sister Fidela would spend some time in the garden tending the vegetable patch that was near the flowers.

They would pick tomatoes and blue berries and dig up carrots. These fruits and vegetables were sent to the kitchen to provide condiments for the recipe of the cook.

When the sun went down, Ava and Sister Fidela would join the other nuns in the chapel to sing some hymns and to say the vespers. It was a bucolic setting somewhere in the hills far away from the hustle and bustle of the city life.

Ava and Sister Fidela would take care of the garden bringing buckets of water from the well and delicately sprinkle them on the plants.

With more than enough sunlight and nutrients from the soil, the plants grew to considerable height. In the fall, the gardener would rake the leaves so that the ground would be exposed to the sunlight and would be fertilized by the rain. He would also trim the bushes with scissors that would take the shape of a square.

There was a small shed in the garden with a small window where the sunlight filtered through.

The gardener kept his tools there, as well as saplings of trees that he intended to plant in the spring. The gardener was hired by the convent to make sure the garden grew in abundance. He was a well-built man who had swarthy looks which made it seem like he had some native American ancestry. He had knobby fingers which made it easier to handle plants.

One day in the middle of spring, Ava went for a stroll in the garden and unfurled her hair to freshen it with some cool wind. Then she felt a tug at her back, and she turned around to see what it was. Before she could say anything, a strong arm grabbed her from the back, and the other hand covered her mouth to prevent her from screaming. In a fast motion, the man dragged her into the shed and tied her hands up and wound a handkerchief around her mouth. She was struggling to break loose, but the man was stronger and heavier than her. The door of the shed was shut, and there were stifled cries and painful groans emanating from within.

She saw with her two eyes the beastly face of the man who violently subdued her. He fondled her breasts and torridly kissed her on the lips. Ava tried to look away, but the man took hold of her head and licked her face with his tongue. He then lifted her skirt, but Ava tried to keep her knees together. However, the man was persistent, and he forced the legs apart and thrust his erect pecker into her middle.

The man bobbed up and down until he reached climax. Ava's throat let out a howling sound indicative of the pain she was going through. It was all over. The man having satiated himself untied Ava and left her disconsolate and forlorn.

Ava covered herself and took out the gag from her mouth. She slowly stood up letting out a shrill cry from the back pain. She crossed the garden and went in the direction of the sleeping quarters. Her hair was disheveled, and her clothes were tattered. There were traces of dirt on her habit. She met Sister Fidela there who was taking a nap. Ava woke her up and hugged her, sobbing like a lost lamb. Sister Fidela asked her where she had been and why her dress was ripped. Ava with a tremulous voice told her that she had been raped. Sister Fidela sat up on the bed and tried to comfort her. She told Ava that they have to report this to the police right away so that the culprit doesn't get away. The Mother Superior has to be informed too so that everyone is waryabout who they're accepting into the monastery. Ava told Sister Fidela that it was the gardener who did this to her.

"Maybe you took off your bandana and started flirting with the gardener," asked Sister Fidela who doubted Ava's version of the story. Ava vehemently denied the allegations and said she was just taking a leisurely walk in the garden when the gardener sneaked up from behind and overpowered her.

They reported the incident to the Mother Superior who called the police. An arrest was made three days later.

Right after the incident, Ava took a hot shower to wipe away the impurities from her body. She built a sudsy lather from soap and shampoo to wash away the dirt, and the grime encrusted on her skin. Also to wash away the sticky sweat and the stale breath of the man who defiled her, from the crown of her head to the soles of her feet. She employed a strong fragrant douche to the inner folds of her middle part to dislodge the excess semen and the filth that violated the vows of chastity she had made upon entering the convent. She never bathed like this before scrubbing repeatedly every inch of her skin to restore its original elasticity.

Afterward, she knelt before the picture of the Madonna to give her strength to forgive her aggressor. But that did not mean the exemption of justice. On the contrary, she would see to it that justice would prevail and that the gardener will be locked up so he could not do this to anyone else.

But then there were doubts in her mind. What if she did show too much skin that instigated the man to act as he did? What if she did show too much of her hair that drove the man wild with desire? She should have heeded the advice of the Mother Superior to cover up her hair. But from then on, the Mother Superior promised not to hire men on the premises.

All the nuns were talking about what happened to the unfortunate nun. They really didn't know who the nun was except that it was one of the sisters. It was fodder for gossip that went around the circle of nuns and leaked out into the world. It seems no one was safe anymore, not even in the confines of a convent. News reports of the incident were carried by various newspapers, but the identity of the victim was not disclosed. The name and address of the rapist was, however, printed in the dailies inviting other possible victims to come forward.

Ava was feeling a little queasy as she sat on a pew and was ready to pray. All of a sudden, Sister Leona sat beside her and launched a litany of accusatory statements directed at Ava. She said, "Women like you belong in a whorehouse. All because of you, the reputation of this convent has been tarnished. I suggest you pack your bags and go back where you came from." Ava was alarmed with what she said and replied with a stern face, "You dim-witted lost soul. You're a witch who has come to question my faith. I won't tolerate your insults." Ava gave Sister Leona a whack on the back. Leona replied with a kick to the buttocks. Ava fell to the ground but came back and pulled the habit out of her hair. The hair of Leona was greasy, black, and full of dreadlocks. Hardly the hair a nun should have.

Leona scratched Ava's face which left marks on her cheeks dripping with blood. The two nuns were yelling obscenities at one another. Then came the other nuns who tried to break up the fight. They separated the two sisters and led them to their cells. Never before has a fight this intense happened in the convent. The sisters will wait for a couple of days to make them cool off. Sister Leona broke the rule of the convent that says one should not reproach a fellow nun and to stay calm amid turbulence. There will be an investigation into the incident, and the offending nun might be expelled. Sister Fidela brought Ava to the appointment with the doctor. They wore street clothes so as not to attract the attention of outsiders. The doctor examined the whole body of Ava. There were bruises and contusions on the thighs, the hips, and the torso. The diagnosis was not good. If left to fester, the tissues would crumple and wither for lack of blood supply. The doctor prescribed her an emollient crème that would improve blood circulation and make the tissues more supple. He also prescribed vitamin C and D to fortify the ligaments. The results of the x-ray were in, and it revealed a fracture in the pelvic bone. Ava needed a cast on her hips that would glue the bones together. The doctor also gave her calcium supplements. As for her feminine functions, Ava could no longer bear children because she was in the menopausal stage. Even if the rapist ejaculated inside her, there was no threat of an unwanted pregnancy. She just have to follow the prescriptions and give it time to heal. As for her mental trauma, the doctor gave her antipsychotic drugs which would fend off the voices she was hearing.

Brian, the son of Ava, was a grown man now. He was still in the custody of his uncle Michael who looked after his needs and ran the household. He knew what happened to his father by reading newspaper clippings and watching reruns of the tragic incident. He was wondering about his mother who he never got to know. He knew she was in a convent, but how she fared by observing a rigorous life, he could only guess. He liked to play soccer with his schoolmates and enjoyed camping out during the long weekends. He carried a picture of his mother in his wallet as he swore that he'd meet her someday. He reserved a room for his mother in the house. He had it painted green with a few paintings by the modern masters on the wall. He put two Oakwood night tables on either side of the bed with bright lamp shades so they could emit enough light. He had the lawn spruced up by planting roses and fir trees. He also hung orchids near the pool. He knew his mother would come home someday. He just didn't know when. If all her wounds would heal, she'll find a comfortable abode waiting for her. She'll find private relaxation in the company of her son and nephews.

His mother was the source of light that would illuminate the dark corners of the house. She would be the glowing embers that would give heat and warmth in a cold wintry night. He did not remember being cradled in her arms, but there was time to make up for it. His heart beat faster by the mere mention of her name. His mother was the missing part of his soul. Every time he shut his eyes at night, he'd dream of her at the center of the solar system radiating love and compassion. Brian knew exactly what to say to his mother in case they let her out of the convent. He will not dwell in the niceties of life or delve into the reason for her isolation. For him, the convent was like a prison camp where women were forced to perform menial tasks and kneel on hard floors while reciting a lengthy prayer. He heard stories about nuns who had to dig up drains so that the sewage will not be clogged. The convent was like a farming community where women had to fix broken pumps and water faucets manually. He just hoped his mother didn't have to undergo a hard life.

Brian can show off his culinary skills to his mother, which he learned at a vocational training center. There are many awesome things he can do with a wok. He can fry crushed garlic in corn oil so that would give a tantalizing aroma to the food. He can sauté vegetables like okra, broccoli, and red peppers so they serve as side dishes to the main course. He also bought a deep frying machine where he immerses chicken drumstick and thigh in vegetable oil to give it a crispy taste. Handling the oven is an easy task for him where he'll cook slabs of pork marinated with lemon sauce to a high heat. He would treat his mother like a queen and give her the comfort that she would be sorely lacking in the cramped quarters of the convent. Here she can spend hours just staring at the window hoping for the heavenly kingdom to descend upon her. There are no limits to what she can do in the privacy of her own home. She can meditate on the mysteries of the rosary retracing the significant events of the New Testament. She can defrock herself of the nun's habit and revert back to the luxurious life. All she has to do is to take an indefinite leave of absence so she can assume the life of a private citizen.

It was already May when the frost on the ground started to melt and the leaves on the trees began to sprout. The flowers in the garden were blooming in full swing as the birds built their nests on the branches. That night Ava retired early in her chamber after a day pottering around the garden meditating on the beauty of nature. She dressed in her nightgown and removed the veil from her hair. She made the sign of the cross and gently snuggled into the blanket and pillows. She was fast asleep. While in a deep slumber, she had a vision of an angel telling her something. The angel had wings and clothing that was dazzlingly white. The angel told her not to be afraid but that he was sent by God to transmit some important information. The angel said that the water in the well had celestial powers and could heal many kinds of maladies. All one had to do was to drink it because it was water that ran along the subterranean river of life. He suggested that the water be poured in small plastic vials and be blessed by the priest for additional reinforcement. The nuns can also filter the water to get rid of contaminants and then distribute the blessed water among the weak and sick parishioners.

The angel also told her that her days in the convent were numbered because her life in the outside world would make a turn for the better. Her mission in the convent was about to end. He instructed her to pray frequently and to receive Holy Communion. By morning, Ava woke up and sat upright in her bed. She remembered her dream vividly and vowed to relay the message to the Mother Superior. She put on her habit and immediately looked for the Mother Superior. Ava told the Mother Superior about the dream, and she believed in the veracity of the narration. She instructed the nuns to do what the angel told Ava and to distribute the water in the chapel. But why was Ava chosen to be the bearer of such good news? Surely there are a lot of sick people out there who could profit from this miraculous water. People who were hopeless cases and had no chance of recuperating. Here is the case of unexplained therapeutic powers that would defy the logic of science and medicine. Perhaps it was the unfortunate events in Ava's life that made her a perfect vessel for the transmission of the article of faith. Whatever it was, people with lifelong illnesses were suddenly cured of their disease. They gave generously to the coffers of the church, and the convent prospered.

The trust that people had in the church was restored, and there was a huge turnout for Sunday mass. People brought their sick relatives to the church and consumed the blessed water with abiding faith. Agnostics who had abandoned the church due to stupor or disenchantment suddenly faced the church with renewed interest. Somehow the magical properties of the water rekindled their faith in the church. The influence of the church grew far and wide. Never before have legions of devotees repented of their sins and listened to the Word of God. All because of Ava's inspired reading by a visit from an angel. The nuns of the Carmelite convent were hailed by the press as the new saviors of the human race. Due to their observance of prayer and fasting, they were able to delve into the mystical sphere of religion. They did the heavenly will of God on earth as they communed with spiritual beings that were invisible to the naked eye. Many people flocked to the convent to seek rest and to be cured of their terminal illness. They were inspired by the frugal life of the nuns and their power to heal wounds. All the nuns had nothing to hide, and their lives inside the convent were well documented. But they were averse to publicity and shunned the invasion of the press.

Ava reflected upon the latter part of what the angel told her. It is true that she had some unfinished business in the outside world. It has already been a long time since she was in the convent and she had no word from her son. How was he doing, and how was he faring in life? She took solace in the company of Sister Fidela who prayed with her to alleviate her grief and anxiety. A priest would say mass at the chapel of the convent every day. Ava would always light a candle and pray for the conversion of wayward souls. Life in the convent has made her more wary of people around her. She could discern the personalities and traits of their other nuns by simply having a chat with them. She used tact and diplomacy when approaching her colleagues to pardon her for some indiscretion. She knew she was far from perfect but counted on the other nuns to be patient with her shortcomings. Living in a community meant that the nuns had to observe table manners and be polite to one another. They were not to vent out emotions of rage which could disrupt the tranquility in the convent. But most of all, the nuns should not indulge in idle chatter. The order of the day was to observe silence and to pray.

Brian was longing to see his mother even if it meant bending the rules. No outsider was allowed to visit the nuns unless it was very important. News from the city was greatly discouraged in order for the nuns to be immersed in prayer and holiness. The convent was a piece of heaven that was cut off from terrestrial links so that the nuns could communicate with God without the least bit of interference. They prayed for the divine intervention of the angels so that they could be united with the holy souls of purgatory. They wanted to be cleansed of their sins because their life on earth was deemed fleeting and temporary. Ava had exhausted all the necessary means to come out on top of the situation. But it seems the nuns gave her a cold shoulder every time she could come up with a suggestion. Her life of prayer was going very well as she learned by rote how to say the rosary. Often she could hardly understand the meaning of the prayers because they were done in a repetitive way. She could see no tangible results and feel no sympathy from the other nuns. A flower that gives off a scent should be put in a vase for everyone to enjoy and not to be left alone to wither. Many times she felt like this flower, ignored and forgotten.

Brian stepped on the gas pedal and accelerated in the direction of the convent which was located in the outskirts of the city. He didn't know what to expect, whether they'll let his mother out or they'll just brush aside his request and hold it in abeyance. He hadn't seen her in twenty years, and the feeling of longing has been building up all these years. What if she was a changed woman and did not recognize her son? Surely there was enough maternal instincts left in her to embrace the full feature of her offspring. By entering the convent, she renounced all links to the outside world. Was she ready to assume the role of mother again? There was an opulent home waiting for her. She could plunge into a Jacuzzi and soak her tired muscles in the luxuriant waters. Or she can splash in the refreshing waters in the pool doing freestyle from one end to the other. This scenario was vastly different from the one she presently lived in. Would she be able to recant her vows and attend to the pressing need of being the lady of the house? She did not fritter away the wealth her husband left her. She knew her son would look for these accessories as a rightful heir. Now that her son had grown up, he wanted to share the material wealth he inherited.

Brian was at the steps of the convent and rang the doorbell. There were nuns huddled near the door wondering who it was that came calling before their noonday prayers. One of them opened the door and was face-to-face with a blond young man who was well-built and dressed casually. He introduced himself and said he was looking for Ava. All the nuns knew who she was and ushered him to the office of the Mother Superior. The Mother Superior was rummaging through her papers when she was interrupted by the young gentleman. She asked, "What can I do for you?" The young man replied that he came to pick up his mother and bring her home. Immediately, the Mother Superior asked the nuns to look for Ava. The nuns gathered around Ava and told her her son had come looking for her. Ava wondered whether this was the answer to her prayer for a respite from the rough and tumble existence in the convent. Upon entering the bureau, she quickly hugged her son and thanked him for his concern. Brian kissed her on the cheek and told her to pack her bags and come home with him. Ava could hardly believe how tall he was since he was only a toddler when she left him. But what of the vows she made? The sisters in the convent would greatly be disappointed if she left in the final stages of her formation.

Her departure would mean one voice less in the recitation of prayers. Surely she couldn't turn her back on the gains she made as a nun joining in the chorus of religious recruits. The four corners of the convent served as a base where she acquired the inclination to detach herself from worldly possessions. Yet here was her son, her own flesh and blood, who was calling out to her to return to her rightful place. Sister Fidela gave her a hug and prompted her to do what her heart told her to do. The Mother Superior nodded at the tearful reunion between mother and son and said she was free to leave the premises. After some serious thought, Ava told her son that she was leaving her life at the convent to be by the side of her young son. Many years have kept them apart, and it was time to mend the gaps that resulted from her absence. She would once again be the feminine figure who would restore order in the household and provide spiritual nourishment to a son that needed it. The family portrait would once again be complete with a new addition to the same roof. No more will the son search vainly for the person who was the source of love and affection. She would be right beside him giving words of encouragement and supplying the strength to move forward.